UNEXPECTED ENGAGEMENT

BABA YAGA'S INSPIRED ROMANCE AND MYSTERY ROLEPLAYING

JOANNA MAZURKIEWICZ

Copyright © 2023 by Joanna Mazurkiewicz

All rights reserved.

No part of this book may be reproduced in any form or by any electronic or mechanical means, including information storage and retrieval systems, without written permission from the author, except for the use of brief quotations in a book review.

YAGA'S CHOICE

BABA YAGA'S LEGACY SERIES
PREQUEL NOVELLA

YAGA'S CHOICE

BABA YAGA'S
LEGACY SERIES
[PREQUEL NOVELLA]

USA TODAY BESTSELLING AUTHOR
JOANNA MAZURKIEWICZ

CHAPTER 1
JADWIGA

"What are you doing, sis? We should get going. He's gonna be here very soon," my best friend mumbled again, watching me pacing around the small alcove inside the church.

My future husband, the man I'd carefully selected for me, was for some reason not here yet, so I was a little concerned. He was never late and normally he had a whole entourage of people with him—witchlords, witches, and other creatures that took care of all his needs and used magic to make his life more comfortable. I'd picked Eric because he was handsome, wealthy, and from a line of pure-blooded magical folk. He held a high rank in the Council and garnered respect far and wide—a perfect match for me.

I was getting nervous, but at the same time I was super excited because my dream of becoming a mother would finally come to pass. My father had helped me arrange it all. The best part was, although Eric's magical skills were extraordinary, there was room for improvement. No one realised that I was on the path of becoming one of the most powerful witches in the Kingdom of Opana.

"You're worrying too much!" she went on. "Eric will be here. I know he's been waiting for this moment. He's probably running late." My friend placed her hand on my back. She was using her magic to make me feel better, but I wasn't sure if that was helping at all.

Witches and witchlords were resentful of my potion-making skills and my father was not pleased with me taking the role of the headmistress of the Academy of Magic in the heart of Lviv. He never wanted me to be a teacher.

Now, here I was, being the dutiful daughter. But this would be good for me. I had a feeling that maybe someone was attempting to sabotage this wedding. My father constantly told me that I had been wasting my talent in the academy, but I relished being surrounded by young witches and witchlords.

It was the summer of 1990. Mortals had their challenges and their technology and science were progressing, but for witches, white magic was the only solution when it came to infertility.

Many believed there was no problem, that there were enough magically-gifted children being born every day, but some witches struggled to conceive. Although a rare occurrence, a few children of mortals also showed signs of being born with magic in the first few days of life.

My father once told me about the prophecy that was spoken by Mokosh, the goddess of fertility. She said that at some point in the future, the entire magical world would be disturbed by the curse and there would be ever fewer children born with magical gifts. This would eventually lead to the death of magic. Apparently, all the gods believed that a mortal witch would grow in power, and she could bring the destruction of order and eventually, the end of magic.

I didn't know if I wanted to believe in such a tale for I

wanted to do the opposite of this—to let magic spread and flourish, not destroy it. Why would any witch wish to destroy that which gives her power?

Besides, there had been many prophecies over the years, and none of them ever came true. Many witches and even witchlords claimed they had seen Perun entering the mortal realm, warning about the use of dark magic, but I knew better. Gods didn't concern themselves with mortals and their problems.

Several weeks ago, when I was in the library getting books to study for the potion I wanted to make tonight, three witches approached me. Two were from the academy, but I didn't recognise the third one. Dagmara was teaching Alchemy, so it was probably her student.

"Principal Jadwiga, we don't want to disturb you, but we need your help," Dagmara said shyly, looking around to make sure no one could hear us. I closed my book and gave her an encouraging smile to continue.

"What can I do for you, Dagmara?" I asked, but I could already sense what she might need as the word in Lviv had spread fast. I didn't like bringing too much attention to myself, but I was already known in the community, amongst other witches and creatures, as a fertility witch.

"This is Veronica. She came all the way from Romania. Can you use your gift, please? She has been trying to conceive for years and since you touched Aneczka—"

"I'm pregnant, Principal Jadwiga. I can't believe it. Every healer and witch has always told me I couldn't have children. This is a miracle and I have you to thank for it," Aneczka said excitedly, loud enough for a few witchlords to hear and turn in our direction. I kept my composure still, but her words sank into me like the claws of a bies demon. She looked so happy, so radiant, and I kept wondering why she was blessed with a child and yet, I remained unable to conceive.

Why on earth had the gods blessed me with this incredible gift that worked on other witches, but not on me?

"That is great news, Aneczka," I said, but deep down I resented her. I was sad and angry that I couldn't get my miracle baby. That witch wasn't any more deserving than I.

I got up and rounded my table, remembering how much Veronica wanted to have a child, so I touched her. I ran my hand over her ovaries and used my energy to heal whatever damage was inside them. I knew that in a few weeks, Dagmara would come to me, thanking me for everything and telling me that Veronica was pregnant.

That was all there was to it. All I had to do, as the witch of fertility, was to touch them.

None of this was fair and I still didn't understand this power that brewed inside me. Some called it the ember of life, but I didn't think that was my true purpose.

It was a very special gift, but for me it was a curse. I was a powerful witch in the kingdom of Opana; it took me a long time to get where I was. I had travelled extensively, learning magic from all sorts of creatures, Slavic demons that no one had ever seen before. I had gone to Siberia to learn about midwifery magic by mamunas. Humans didn't know about magic, but our worlds had always been connected. I had no idea why they remained so ignorant.

"Jadwiga, he's here! Let me help you with the dress," Kasia said, pulling me away from my thoughts. It took me a moment to remember that today was my wedding day.

Kasia started ushering me closer towards the doors, after she stopped peering through them.

She was super pumped that I finally decided to settle down. We had known each other for years. We grew up together back in Lviv and she was my best friend, but Kasia had no idea about my involvement in dark magic. No one in my circle would understand or accept it, especially her family. I knew that it bothered her that I was always so ambitious and brave.

After dipping my toes into dark magic and forbidden spells, I stopped talking to her about my work. I had done unforgivable things and used magic that no one else had access to. If anyone from the Council found out, I knew I would burn for it.

"Are you sure that's him?" I asked, nervous. I was very good at masking my emotions, so it felt odd that I was suddenly so anxious.

Eric had no idea that he was helping me with any of it. By simply consummating our marriage, my magic would grow. Afterwards, I had to complete brewing an ancient and complicated potion, the Flask of Nightmares.

Once the potion was ready, Eric would drink it and then I would finally break the curse and be able to conceive.

"Of course it's him. Who would it be otherwise?" Kasia laughed, staring at me and probably wondering what was wrong with me and why I was asking such silly questions. "Hurry up dear, everyone is waiting."

She gave me a warm smile and then quickly vanished. Moments later, there was a light knock and my father walked in. He was a tall, slender man with blond hair. We were very much alike in facial features.

I didn't remember my mother but Dad often told me she'd been incredibly beautiful. From photographs I'd seen of her, I didn't note any resemblance with her. She was blond, tanned, and petite, whereas I had brown hair, a tall, lean body, and fair skin.

"You look absolutely stunning, my dear daughter. Eric is such a lucky man," my father said proudly. Warmth spread across my chest at his compliment. He was always so firm and harsh. In the past, everything I had ever done or achieved was never good enough for him, but today he seemed truly pleased that I'd finally decided to get married.

He walked up to me and took my hand, ready to walk me to the altar. Then he muttered something under his breath and the door opened.

I had chosen this venue because it was small, intimate, and the old church had a rich history. One of the councillors was going to officiate the ceremony.

My heart pounded inside my chest with every step we took. The music started playing and everyone turned to look at me.

Eric was waiting for me at the altar. I told myself that I needed to relax. He looked a bit taller from a distance, and much broader.

Suddenly, an unfamiliar feeling of dread spread through my core and I inhaled sharply. My magic zoomed around the church. I knew some of these witches and witchlords were resentful of me, of the fact that Councillor Eric had chosen me as his life partner.

A few of my cousins looked happy for me, but witches hailing from more distant family were scared of me. Everyone here was aware of my growing power, but no one would dare challenge me.

Despite being so young, I'd already been with many witchlords. I enjoyed having sex but at the end of the day, none of those men could get me pregnant.

I had gone to many healers and witches, but no one could ever figure out what was wrong with me. They also told me I had a blood disease, that my magic was tainted, so they couldn't help me. Devastated, I forged on, looking for a solution.

Tonight, I would be able to conceive because the Flask of Nightmares would kill my new husband. Eric had no clue that he was going to die tonight and at this point, I didn't really care. Accidents happened and I could cover my tracks so no one suspected a thing. His family would probably hate me, but I was willing to sacrifice him for the greater good.

After taking forever walking towards the altar, I was finally standing next to Eric. My father smiled at him and let me go. I watched him as he took his seat in the front row. Then, my husband-to-be finally turned to look at me and in that moment I realised that the man I was going to marry wasn't Eric.

CHAPTER 2
JADWIGA

This man who stood next to me was much taller and broader than Eric. I noticed this earlier on but dismissed it, chalking it up to nerves. My belly made a flip.

The stranger was so very handsome. He had a strong jaw and kissable lips. His long, dark brown hair was pulled in a ponytail. When I finally looked him directly in the eyes, I realised that he was neither witchlord nor human. He couldn't have been because the power inside him threatened to make me explode, spreading everywhere like wildfire. I had never felt anything like it.

I glanced around, feeling apprehensive and confused. Why had no one reacted? Everybody was just staring at us as though everything was absolutely fine.

"Who are you?" I hissed at the stranger, sensing his strength. "Where is Eric?"

He smiled, arching his left eyebrow as he trailed his gaze to my lips, then down past my cleavage and the rest of my body. My pulse quickened in reaction and heat rushed to my core. I was ready to pull out my wand and chant a spell, but my energy felt silent.

Something was seriously wrong.

"Calm down, Jadwiga. You have to be yourself; otherwise people will suspect there is something wrong," he said, his voice smooth like velvet, sending a tremor down my spine. I didn't recognise his accent, but he spoke in Slovenian—a common language in the Kingdom of Opana.

I swallowed thickly and glanced at the councillor who was conducting the ceremony, but he was busy looking down at his book. He seemed completely unfazed by the fact that my groom had been replaced by a complete stranger who was using dark magic. I was certain he'd spellbound everyone in the church and made them believe he was Eric.

"This is unacceptable. I'm not going to marry you. Who are you? And where is Eric? What did you do to him?"

"That's a lot of questions, Jadwiga, so let's start with the simple one." The stranger chuckled. "My name is Veles and I am God of the Underworld."

My lips parted but no words could come out of my mouth.

"No… this isn't happening. I have this whole thing planned out. I won't let you ruin this for me," I hissed.

Veles took my hand and squeezed it. His energy rushed through my heart and then through every cell in my body, filling me with ecstasy. I gasped, feeling as if struck by thunder and lightning. The god of the underworld stood right in front of me, if I had to believe him. His power certainly confirmed it.

Normally, gods didn't interfere in human or witch affairs. So what was happening here?

"You can't force me to marry you."

The god dragged his hand across his chin, never breaking his intense stare.

"Oh yes, I can and I will. You will obey me now or I will kill all your family and friends gathered here today. Am I making myself clear?"

My heart threw itself over my ribcage as I continued to stare at him. This wasn't happening to me—especially not now when I was so close to getting what I wanted.

I wet my dry lips and scanned the space. My father sat with his hand on his heart, eyes shut. Something was wrong with him and I started to panic.

Why was this man, this *god*, even here and why was he hijacking my wedding. Was this a punishment for every bad thing I'd done in the past?

"Why me? I'm insignificant," I insisted. "A nobody."

"You're very important, Jadwiga, and you're going to help me. So let's begin," he said. "I'd discovered your secret. Your're able to create life and destroy me—the immortal."

I didn't understand anything what he said. I didn't have such a gift.

"You're wrong about me."

"Councillor Robert closed his book and looked alert, all of a sudden. He smiled at us and said it was time to proceed. I called out for my magic, to no avail. This eternal being had just confirmed that he needed my help—or my submission, more like. I had to hope that Veles wasn't planning to stay married to me for long.

I trembled with anger and resentment. So much planning gone down the drain. In order for my potion to work, I needed Eric. I had no idea what this stranger had done to him, but everything I had worked for my entire life was just about to be ruined.

"Witches and witchlords of Opana, we are gathered here today to celebrate the marriage of Eric and Jadwiga," the councillor spoke, so everyone went quiet.

I wanted to disappear and pretend that this wasn't happening. The room teemed with excitement. Kasia was beaming through her tears, none the wiser like the rest of them.

I felt paralysed by his magic, by my inability to do anything. The councillor went on with the usual wedding spiel. Then, the choir of witches sang a few songs that Eric and I had specifically picked for our special day.

Finally, it was time to take our vows.

"Jadwiga, repeat after me," the councillor requested. "I take you, Eric Kozak, to be my lawful husband and promise to the true to you in good times and in bad, in sickness and in health. I will love you and honour you all the days of my life."

I felt sick to my stomach but repeated the vows while Veles squeezed my hand. He seemed so calm and relaxed. I never thought I would be in this situation, trapped by a god. This felt like a nightmare I didn't know I could ever wake from.

"You have declared your consent before the Church. May the Lord in His goodness strengthen your consent and fill you both with His blessings. What God has joined, men must not divide. Amen."

Veles seemed to approve because his expression said so. I was breathing through my nose, telling myself that I wasn't going to be sick. It was a done deal. We were bound to each other now and my only chance of becoming a mother was lost forever.

"You may kiss the bride."

I was ready to make an escape, but I couldn't move. Veles' dark, penetrating eyes were staring down at me.

No way was I going to kiss him. I was ready to scream and stop him from coming closer, but then I thought about my poor father and everyone else. I couldn't let him hurt them.

The gorgeous god of the underworld stared at me with hunger and need. It couldn't be that bad, could it? I swallowed hard, telling myself to stay calm.

And then, overwhelming waves of energy and tingles broke

over my whole body, igniting my magic. He moved closer, then his hand was on my waist and I was staring at my own reflection in his incredible eyes. Before I could react to stop him in some way, his lips touched mine, softly at first. When he brought me closer, explosive lust rippled through me.

My head spun as he devoured my mouth, tasting like dark night and red wine. His energy took root in every nook and cranny of my body, spreading like warm chocolate. When he pulled back, I was lost to these incredible sensations that rocked through me.

Then I realised the whole church was cheering. Moments later, I was being dragged away from the altar with magic so strong, I felt as if pulled in different directions.

"Congrats, hon! I am crying… why am I even crying?" Kasia rambled on while this god, Veles, held my hand.

I had to be dreaming…

"Let go of me now. We aren't married. This didn't happen for real," I spat as we got outside the church.

We were in the human part of the city so magic here was limited, but this church was special to me. It was where my parents got married—and now, so had I.

"Of course it was real. You're my wife, dear Jadwiga. I came here on Earth to take you as my bride and to defeat my brother, Perun. You're my secret and most precious weapon."

CHAPTER 3
VELES

She was supposed to be strong, to be my weapon, but she was weak. I came to Earth under the impression she would be the answer to all my problems. She was able to create life and destroy immortals. I entered the human realm through the secret gate. My brother, Svarog, had shown me how to use the firelight magic to cross over from Nawia.

I didn't want to believe in the prophecy that all the other creatures were whispering about, but I sensed that taking this human witch could truly work to my advantage when it came to Perun.

My brother had overstayed his usefulness. His constant threats to my power and position in the underworld were not to be taken lightly. Perun wanted it all—and I was here to stop him. Destroying him was the only option. If I didn't, I'd always be looking over my shoulder, expecting the worst.

So, to that end, I married this woman without hesitation. Our union would produce an alliance and her ultimate sacrifice would rid me of the bane of my existence.

She was a powerful witch; I could sense that, but no match for me. This realm was so different from what I was used to.

Humans didn't know about magic and the affairs of witches. They were all walking around and living their lives unaware of what was happening around them.

The wedding was underwhelming, but I planned to enjoy my time with her. She had no idea what I had prepared for her later on.

We headed straight to the reception venue in a building located in the heart of the forest, where the guests gathered in a large hall. The place was so beautiful, with a small lake in the distance, surrounded by exquisite nature. I'd hang around here as long as I could.

My bride was tense and nervous. She kept staring at me with a mixture of fear and anger, constantly mumbling spells under her breath.

She already hated me and I was okay with that, since I'd have to sacrifice her in the end. This was all about the energy I could use to finally defeat my brother. With this in mind, I still needed to figure out how much power this woman possessed. The essence of immortality resided within her but she was blinded by her ambition.

"How long are you planning to keep me in your magical prison, married to you?" she asked bluntly.

"I'm not sure yet, but it will be for as long as I need to," I replied.

People found their seats and so did we, at our table by the front of the building. Servants entered carrying trays laden with food and drinks.

I noticed that my wife was drinking heavily. She seemed intoxicated by the alcoholic beverages that were placed in front of us.

"What?" she asked with wide eyes. Her chest rose and fell in rapid movements. "Why are you staring? You can't do this to me. Soon, all these people will realise you're not Eric. You can't keep them in a trance forever."

She seemed to be considerably irritated by my presence, and that made her more attractive to me. Something brewed between us. I could feel it. Normally I didn't pay attention to these things, but since I was in the human realm, I was more perceptive regarding these new emotions.

Damn shame that I had to kill her. I continued to observe her, sensing her heightened arousal, and her face flushed at my perusal. She liked to be in control, to dominate the male sex, but that wasn't going to happen with me. The sooner she learned, the better.

"No one will know because nobody is able to break my illusion spell. You don't have to worry about anything, so just enjoy yourself because the celebrations will end soon and I will have you all to myself, with no interruptions."

"If you are truly the god of the underworld then why do you need me? I'm just a mortal being. I might be a powerful witch, but I am still insignificant. You must let go of me," she demanded, drawing a laugh from me.

Then I remembered Lucinda's words: she needs to love you and you need to experience mortality in order to conquer your brother. Otherwise, your new power won't manifest in this realm.

So maybe killing her wasn't a solution and the truth was, I didn't want to end her life.

"No, I won't let go of you. We are going to stay together for now, so it will be better if you just get used to me. Tell me more about yourself. Where are you from and how is your life?" I asked, trying to stay calm, but all I could think about was embracing her and devouring her mouth. Then I would take her upstairs to our new quarters, where I would ravage her, testing her body and soul, and giving her unlimited pleasure.

Obviously disturbed by my questions, she folded her arms over her chest and let out a sharp exhale. I shifted on the chair, trying to control my arousal.

"I was born in Ukraine and from an early age, I always taught others. Teaching and being a leader came naturally to me. I had it in my blood. I was only marrying Eric because I needed to have a baby and now you've ruined everything. He was my vessel, the man I needed in order to conceive. This is what I have always truly desired. So now you know and you can help me. You are the god of the underworld and with your power you can take away my special gift and give me the child. I have helped many infertile women to conceive, but now it's my turn to become a mother."

That was very interesting that this mortal woman wished for so much. I needed to consummate the marriage to unlock the magic, but I didn't think I could conceive a child with her. Gods weren't supposed to reproduce, especially with mortals.

"I don't think this is so simple. You should know that eternal beings cannot create life. Don't worry, Eric is still alive, but he is in another realm," I explained.

Jadwiga's eyes went wide. She was so beautiful, and her desire for power enticed me all the more.

"Well, so you can bring Eric back and I can proceed with my plan," she insisted.

A witch approached our table at that moment. She smiled shyly at me, twirling a lock of her around her finger. I could sense she was a good friend to my wife, Jadwiga, whose lips pursed at the woman's expression.

"It's time for the speeches. Your father will go first," the witch said. Her eyes started twinkling at the corners with magic. She wanted to say something else, but she hesitated.

"Is there anything else?" I asked

"Yes, you promised me a dance, my lord," she added, flustered.

Jadwiga looked decidedly annoyed.

"Once I take care of my wife, I will dance with you. Now it's time for you to go back to your table to listen to the speech. Enjoy yourself, mortal woman."

"Kasia will know soon that you're not Eric. He doesn't speak in that manner," Jadwiga stated. "And once your spells fade away, my father will realise what you have done and he won't be happy."

The man in question rose and tapped his fork over a glass, so everyone stopped talking.

As he started speaking, I isolated myself from my body when Svarog appeared in this realm. Nobody noticed him standing in the corner, so I got up and went to him but my body remained present, staring at Jadwiga's father.

"I see, brother, that you achieved what you intended. The woman is beautiful. Have you figured out how to make her useful to you?" he questioned me, staring around at all the mortals. The flames around his body burned brightly.

"She desires to give birth to a child. This is going to be a challenge, but we both know gods cannot create life," I explained. "I need her to desire me, to make her love me in order to activate the magic that could kill my brother."

Svarog shook his head and chuckled. "You are selfish. You never took care of anyone before, so I don't think you can make her fall in love with you, brother."

I dragged my hands through my hair, not wanting to agree with him, but he was right. I took care of the lost souls. I had done anything I'd ever wanted—taken lovers, made sure my needs were always met, but this was something else. This woman didn't want me for who I was, so I had to show her I could look after her, that I could be good for her.

"I have faith in my seductive abilities but I need some time with her," I said, certain that after two human weeks, I could make her love me.

I reached out to shake his hand and smiled. My brother had seduced many mortal women, but like me, he'd never experienced love. I had been told that this emotion wasn't for us to know or even understand.

"You have to impress her because you can't force her to be with you. It has to come from her," he said as we shook hands.

"I'm aware of what I need to do. You don't have to school me. I'll make her desire and love me, so you have my word. Now it's time for you to oversee me."

With that, I returned to my body. Jadwiga's father was just about to end his speech. Everybody was clapping and my new wife appeared to be moved by his words. I placed my hand on her arm and she tensed instantly. Svarog was right in a way—this wasn't going to be easy. But Jadwiga was open-minded. I had to prove she needed me more than she realised.

I tapped on my champagne glass. This wasn't the time for my speech, but I had to put my plan in motion, so I proceeded to get everyone's attention. Jadwiga's expression turned to surprise. I put my hand over hers and stood.

"Thank you, everybody, for coming today. This was a special and magical ceremony. My wife looked absolutely stunning and I'm so lucky she chose me to be her new partner in life. I feel privileged to support her in her important work at the academy. We are from different worlds, but we understand each other. I promise I will give her everything she ever wanted, especially the family that she so desires."

The seduction process was going to be long and complicated, but I was certain I could ask Mokosh to make Jadwiga a mother, and give her the child she desperately wanted.

"I'm standing next to her as her companion, as her lover and teacher, ready to spend the rest of my life with her. We met in Russia and spent so many wonderful times together. When she was attacked by a demon, I saved her life and in that moment I knew I couldn't let her go. I was there when she needed a shoulder to cry on, when she came back to the country and was afraid to face her family. I encouraged and motivated her. We shall remain together until death do us part."

People started clapping and cheering for me, and a few women even shed a tear or two. I took her hand and kissed her. She wasn't impressed, nor surprised that I was privy to such an important detail from her life. It was easy for me to read her thoughts.

"Great speech, but I still want Eric back. I need him for the potion I created."

"Why are you so interested in that mortal? Eric isn't relevant and I could help you with your potion. We could use each other. Let's make a deal with each other," I said. I just needed a little time to show her I was the one she wanted. She didn't even know that yet, but I was seeing myself with her in the future. The plan to kill her was fast fading away.

"All right, let's make a deal. You help me to brew the potion and bring me human essence—the one ingredient I am missing —and then I will help you bring your brother down," she agreed.

Now I understood. She wanted to kill Eric and use his essence for the potion. This was an unexpected twist.

"I don't understand why you need to have a child. All I can see is your desire for power. You are going to be the greatest witch in the Kingdom of Opana, feared by many—and you will lead your people to greatness," I said, looking into her future. She was cruel and unpredictable, but she was cherished by so many other witches and witchlords. As I told her, she was born to be a leader.

"I want to be a mother. This has always been my greatest

dream. Apparently, our family line was cursed and my mother was the last woman who could ever conceive a child. If this is true, then you must help me break the curse and take away my gift," she pledged, moving closer. The warmth of her body was suddenly distracting. "So now, let's go upstairs to consummate our marriage."

I stared at her lips, inhaling the scent of her arousal. The blood in my veins was filled with heat. Jadwiga was a beautiful woman, but she was trying to manipulate me with her desire.

Suddenly, the wedding guests started cheering for us. They were shouting "*Goszko!*" and lifting their glasses in toast to us. Jadwiga smiled at me, then she leaned over and whispered in my ear.

"It's time for you to kiss me again. They all demand it and I have missed your lips, Veles."

CHAPTER 4
JADWIGA

He entangled his hand in my hair and held me in place. I gasped when he brought me closer and kissed me. His lips moved over mine and then I heard more cheering. By the time he pulled away from me, I was breathless and the scorching warm energy was spreading through my core. This giant god was going to make me lose my mind. A small smile danced on his full lips.

The party would go on for another few hours, but I wanted to be alone with Veles.

Kasia had organised everything and the whole ceremony had gone exactly how I imagined it until I realised that Eric had been replaced by the God of the Underworld. I couldn't doubt him. His power was enormous and his energy overwhelming. Now, we just needed to consummate the marriage so he could get me pregnant. He kept saying that he couldn't create life for he was a god. But he could do anything.

He caressed my hand, his fingers warm and soft. I tried to imagine him in Nawia when he was torturing other souls and leading demons to the pits of hell, but the picture never quite formed in my mind. I felt attracted to him, no doubt, but this was yet another distraction. I had never acted on my desires. I used witchlords for sex because I was always afraid to get emotionally attached to anyone.

"What exactly do you want from me, Veles?" I asked.

He smiled, causing the butterflies in my belly to flutter.

"Let's dance. I want you in my arms," he replied. And then he drew me flush to him. The warmth of his body made my magic surface and travel over my skin.

I had never felt like this, despite my anger that he'd taken Eric and jeopardised my plans. The Flask of Nightmares was a difficult alchemic potion to brew. It had taken me much effort and financial investment to get all the ingredients I needed. Besides, I was risking a lot. This kind of magic was forbidden and now it was all going to waste.

"I don't want to dance. I want to go to the bedroom where you promised you'll make love to me, so then I can finally get pregnant," I insisted.

I wasn't even sure if he was able to give me children, but I was willing to do anything to make that a reality. The child would have his genes and powerful magic.

This wasn't common or expected, but the idea of immortality drew me in. Ultimately, this was my goal—to become immortal and so powerful, no one would ever challenge me.

Everyone I'd spoken to in the past had told me that I was playing with fire, that this kind of magic was too dark and twisted. It could trap me in the other realm forever, but I didn't care. I wanted to keep on living.

My father had no idea what I'd been doing in the past several years. With Veles now I had a chance to show everyone what I was truly capable of. My father needed to understand that my position as a teacher would never hold me back.

Veles smiled.

"I want to get to know you first, dear Jadwiga. There will be time for pleasure later," he said, then led me to the dance floor. Everyone else was having a great time, none the wiser. My father was dancing with a witch, which surprised me. Perhaps Veles' magic affected him, too. Once more, Veles brought me closer to his enormous body, his eyes gleaming with lust, then placed his hand on my waist and started moving to the rhythm of the music.

He was surprisingly gentle and I was shocked that he knew how to dance. I would have thought he wasn't familiar with the mortals' way of life.

"When did you learn how to dance?"

The anger had subsided, even though the Flask of Nightmares situation lingered in my mind. I sensed he wanted this—to work something out with me. Crazy but true.

"Once I stepped into this realm, all earthly knowledge became available to me," he explained.

"Interesting," I muttered, wondering if he could salvage my potion. There was still time, but I had to go back to my home soon and check on it.

"Is something bothering you, Jadwiga?" he asked.

His musky scent filled my nostrils then. So arousing…

"Yes, I left a brewing potion at home and need to tend to it right away," I admitted then quickly added, "You can help me. I will take you there, so you can speed up the brewing time. How about making everyone pass out drunk and let's leave?"

Veles held me in a firm grasp as we moved around the dance floor. My breathing was erratic and our closeness made me feel wild things for him.

"Hmm, you're very tempting, woman. Fine, I can take you back to your potion, but first you have to promise to let me show you who I am," he whispered in my ear.

What did he mean by letting him show me who he was?

"Fine, Veles. This is yet another deal but I accept your terms," I said, hopeful. Maybe everything wasn't lost just yet.

"That's great news, mortal woman, but I am enjoying dancing with you. This is rather pleasing."

He was so close and I wished he'd kiss me again. I floated on the dance floor as he practically carried me and spun me around. I didn't miss how other witches stared at him. His spell was strong, but they were all noticing that he was something more than the witchlord Eric. Although he took on the man's appearance in their eyes, there was something different about him. He was broader and bigger, his jaw more defined.

My attraction grew with every moment. I relished his closeness and couldn't deny it.

By the time the dance ended I was breathless, hot and bothered. Soon, we'd cut the cake and go through the other silly newlywed rituals.

I went back to my table and plopped down on the chair, hoping he'd spirit me away soon. I closed my eyes for a moment, soothing my impatience, and when I opened them again, everyone and everything had vanished.

All the wedding guests, the venue, and the music were gone, replaced by a large bedroom with a four-poster bed in the middle of it.

I glanced around, trying to understand what had happened.

"Where are we?" I asked.

"In our marital suite. Don't worry; the guests are still enjoying themselves," he explained, watching me intensely.

"But surely, people will notice that we aren't there?"

"I made them all intoxicated by alcohol and magic, so no one will remember a thing. They will recall the good times, including the ceremony. Everything is fine," he assured me.

I nodded, though filled with uncertainty. Then I went to the window and pulled back the curtain. Outside, a forest stretched for miles.

"What is this place? It's beautiful," I asked, my potion still at the forefront of my mind. Veles was wasting valuable time.

"It's an old manor house in the heart of Slovenia, far from any human villages," he replied. "Let's explore, dearest."

I nodded, feeling oddly calm. It seemed that Veles was making me feel less anxious.

We left the bedroom and headed downstairs through the wide staircase.

The manor house was beautiful, but old. The wooden floor squeaked under our weight. I was certain that a witch or witchlord must have occupied this house in the past, because magic clung to the walls, seeping into all the old paintings and dusty furniture.

Veles took me to the kitchen and I stopped to regroup. This space was also spacious with a huge old chimney stove in the centre of it.

For a moment I allowed my imagination to go wild as I pictured myself there with him, living like a real family. I was busy placing plates on the table while our child played by the door. The powerful vision shook me to the core.

"What are you thinking about?" he asked, bringing me back to reality.

I shook my head and gave him a warm smile.

"About my life," I said, not wanting to disclose the truth. I wasn't even sure if he could read me or not, but this vision freaked me out a little. "I thought you were going to take me back to my place, so I can work on my potion."

"I have everything arranged so we could head over to your potion right away. Just say the word," he teased.

I was a little confused by his conflicting words. What was I to expect? It had taken so much to learn black magic, while keeping all my activities hidden from the world.

"Lead on," I said, and he nodded. Soon enough, we left the kitchen and got to a room below the house via a narrow staircase. I could barely see where I was going until I found myself in a huge open space filled with books. The lighting was dim and there was a large wooden table in the middle. I recognised all my stuff—my mortar, my herbs, magical artefacts and everything I'd left there before heading to the church.

I shuddered thinking about the plastic bag containing the virgin witch's ovaries laid out among all my things there.

I paid a lot of money to acquire these organs. On top of that, the witchlord who'd sold me the ovaries was way too talkative. I had to slit his throat in the end because he was becoming a nuisance.

Veles watched me walking around and the silence stretched for some time. We both needed something from each other. He wanted my magic to conquer his brother and I needed to get pregnant.

It was a simple business arrangement, that's all. I couldn't get emotionally attached to him because he wouldn't be here for long.

"Why don't you ask me about the ovaries? I'm sure you're curious," I said, finally looking at him.

The shock of seeing all my stuff in front of me finally faded. Veles was a god, so he could get inside any home or place he fancied. He stood there looking proud and tall, his long brown hair falling over his shoulder. I couldn't deny it—he was so hot. I wondered if this was his true appearance he showed in Nawia.

My stomach tightened as desire built in the pit of my stomach. My nipples hardened and I wished I would be brave enough to walk over to him and kiss him.

I inhaled sharply and in a flash, he was beside me. I instantly backed against the wall. Reaching out, he brushed a lock of my hair away from my face. He was staring at me like I was his prey.

"I'm not interested in your reasons. I just want to see you working towards your goal. You're very beautiful and right now, I want to kiss you," he said in a husky voice that sent tremors down my spine. I wondered why he was asking for permission. He was a god and shouldn't be concerned about my wishes.

He was obviously also a gentleman. I smiled lightly and licked my upper lip. He was so close, his body only inches away from mine, and a tingling sensation spread between my legs.

"Then why don't you do it already?" I whispered, giggling. What the hell had gotten into me. I was playing with fire and my very life.

The god of the underworld pressed his hard and lean body against mine. I gasped when he grabbed my hands and raised them above my head, keeping them prisoner with his viselike grip. His fiery gaze pinned me down and his warm breath fanned my face.

"You're mine," he growled. "I'm going to taste you now."

"I'm still wait—"

I didn't finish what I wanted to say because he pressed his lips to mine in a violent and urgent kiss. There were plenty of things I wanted to complain about, but he quickly made me forget about them.

His lips were so soft and welcoming. Veles tasted like black cherries and cinnamon. He kissed me hard, melting my insides until my magic vibrated through my core.

I moaned into his mouth when I felt his erection against my navel, then he bit my bottom lip. He finally stopped and pulled away.

"You taste like sugar cane, vanilla, and roses, mortal woman," he rasped, his eyes hooded. "I can't seem to control myself when I'm around you."

I couldn't respond or move. My body pulsated with his magic and I had never been more turned on in my entire life, lost to this frenzy of arousal and excitement. I craved to have him inside me, pushing into me slowly while I moaned for more.

I wasn't supposed to want him. My brain screamed at me to push him away, but my body was too weak to react. My lips felt swollen and abused.

"Let go of me," I hissed. "I should get to work. We are wasting precious time."

"I won't let you go unless you admit you want me."

"I don't want you, Veles. I don't even like you," I scoffed and he chuckled, running his thumb over my lips.

He smiled again, shaking his head.

"You are such a liar, Yaga. Your core is trembling for more of this."

CHAPTER 5
VELES

She was my weakness and would be my end. When I stared at her breathless and hard, I wanted to rip her clothes off and take her, here and now. There was something about Jadwiga that turned me into a beast.

She was beautiful and her feisty nature shone like a beacon. I desired to make her mine. All these new emotions I was experiencing were foreign to me.

Attraction zoomed between us. Her chest was rising and falling in rapid movements as I held her hands.

I wanted to capture her lips, run my hands over her delicate flesh and hear her moaning for me. I yearned to fill her with pleasure. My judgement was clouded and she wasn't innocent. She had used other mortals for her own personal gain.

Jadwiga was determined to become a leader in Opana, but she also wanted to be a mother. She intrigued me…

I pictured her naked body spread on the bed upstairs while I explored her magnificent breasts and the bundle of nerves between her legs.

Her little sounds of pleasure were music to my ears, but she had to confess her desire for me.

She shielded her mind from me using magic, so I couldn't fully read her thoughts. Witches were more advanced than humans. Besides, I wanted to play a fair game.

Her pounding heart echoed in my ears as she stared daggers at me. Anger and desire ... I had no doubt then she wanted me.

She was supposed to be my weapon against my brother, but already, I couldn't see myself hurting her or even ending her life.

"Then fuck me, Veles. What are you waiting for? I want to have you inside me," she said confidently.

I instantly let go of her hands and took a step back. Rage now boiled in my veins. My inner voice kept whispering that this wasn't how my plan was supposed to pan out.

We were both acting out on our desire, but her attitude was something more. If I wanted to use her for her magic, I needed her to submit wholly to me. My cock was hard as a rock and the obsession was real for the first time ever.

Women, mortal and immortal, were always at my disposal. They all came willingly because they were determined to serve me. Back in Nawia, I lived detached from my emotions.

"As much as I want to hear you moaning my name when I fuck you, the time isn't right," I countered. "You said it yourself that you have to concentrate on the potion."

She looked disappointed but after a while, she straightened up and fixed her messy hair.

"You were the one that lost control, not me," she snapped in annoyance.

I inhaled sharply, entertaining the thought of diving right between her legs and making her orgasm like she had never before.

She was right. I had lost control, but she wasn't innocent. She was hoping I would lose focus.

Jadwiga walked over to the table and scanned a page of one of her books. She was even more beautiful when she was trying to concentrate.

She studied the text for several minutes, licking the edge of her thumb and turning the pages.

"Is there a problem?" I asked.

She looked at me and shifted her weight to one side.

"No," she replied, closing the book. "I think you're a little grumpy today, aren't you?"

Fair point. I was grumpy, hungry, and frustrated. All these feelings were somehow exhausting, but I needed to focus on my goal: getting rid of Perun once and for all.

"I'm not used to waiting for anything," I snapped, surprising myself with this new emotion once again.

I wanted to have her in my bed. At the same time, I remembered what I was here for. I wasn't supposed to get emotionally attached to this beautiful creature. In the end, as much as I didn't want this and would tell myself I wasn't going to, she would likely have to be sacrificed in order to for me to gain what I needed.

Soon, Jadwiga started whispering magical formulas and her potion began to boil. She shut her eyes and chanted some spells, then dropped some items inside the liquid. After this, she emptied several colourful flasks into the concoction before moving to the herbs and other things she had spread on the table.

I sensed that this was going to be a long and exhausting night. This potion that she was creating was powerful, reminiscent of the magic that I occasionally used—one that wasn't normally accessible to mortals.

I kept watching her as she worked in silence, wondering if I was cut out for this—waiting for a woman I desired. At last, I picked a few books and read them to pass the time.

This whole process was frustrating but I had to leave her be because this potion was obviously important to her. Two hours later, she huffed and I looked up at her flushed, sweaty face. She had a few dark smudges on her cheeks.

"After I'm done, I just have to brew it for forty-eight hours straight. I might have to stay up all night to keep an eye on it because I only have one chance to get it right. This is dark magic, the sort of energy that should disturb the gods. It's forbidden to witches in Opana," she explained, her tone full of trepidation.

She was right. This magic was rubbing me the wrong way and I had never experienced anything like it.

"I'm not here to judge you. Do what is necessary to achieve your goal," I explained, thinking about my brother. He must have noticed this woman. How could he have not?

She stared at me with a mixture of surprise and pride before wiping the sweat off her forehead.

"I'm not a good person. My soul is tainted," she admitted.

"You had good intentions," I muttered. She was risking a lot. In the Kingdom of Opana, if caught, Jadwiga would have ended up in prison, her magic taken away from her for killing an innocent soul.

"This is my gift, and my curse that this potion could finally break. I paid someone to bring me the organs of the virgin witch no questions asked," she added, sounding suddenly excited.

She started placing several other things inside the mortar, including a rat tail, an eel, and a number of rare herbs. I didn't get involved with human affairs, but I recognised these things from the magical world. It seemed that Jadwiga was experienced in alchemy.

"We aren't in Nawia but in another realm, so again I'm not judging," I said.

She nodded, hesitating for a moment when she picked up the plastic bag. Soon, the virgin witch's ovaries went inside the pot. The mixture began to bubble again. The smell was unpleasant, but Jadwiga kept a keen eye on it as though it were the most precious thing. After a while, the liquid turned black and the smoke started evaporating. I was fascinated by her incredible skills. The dark magic seeped under my skin, spreading slowly and settling in my bones. Normally, I wasn't affected by it, but I was away from Nawia and feeling weakened in this realm.

Jadwiga's body went rigid and then she started levitating, rising above the floor. Her whole body shook as she fell into some sort of trans, her eyes rolling to the back of her head. The potion was brewing slowly, and it had to attach itself to her gift.

I couldn't take away that gift—this wasn't something I could do—but others could probably help her.

In that moment, I wasn't ready to ask for help. The moment I married her, she became my possession to secretly cherish … to keep to myself. Soon, the whole room was covered in thick white smoke.

Jadwiga started panting loudly and moaning as though in pain, her hands still above her head. She glowed, surrounded by a bright red light. The potion continued to boil.

I waved my hand, attempting to imbue her with a bit more strength until she fell to the wooden floor with a thud. The smoke turned dark and started covering her, getting into her lungs and all inside her, disturbing her magic. I remained still, certain she could fight this. We both needed to trust the process.

The potion was resisting and these were the effects. Soon though, it would be all over.

"What's happening? Is that you, Veles?" The feminine voice took me away from Jadwiga.

I turned around as Yaga pushed the darkness away, seeing a woman that materialized on the staircase. I instantly relaxed and smiled. Mokosh, the Goddess of Fertility, had found me here. I shouldn't have been surprised. She always liked to track my movements.

"Welcome, Mokosh. I was hoping that I wouldn't be disturbed by anyone here," I said in amusement.

Mokosh hailed from a deadly realm back in Nawia. She hated my brother Perun with a vengeance and wanted him gone, just like me.

I never shared my plans with her, but she must have found out from someone else that I'd decided to enter the mortal realm, otherwise she wouldn't be here now.

Jadwiga managed to fight off the darkness, the smoke ebbed, but the energy of the potion remained strong. Jadwiga was breathing hard, but she lifted herself off the floor.

"This mortal woman, the witch, is going to help us get rid of my brother. I've made a deal with her. I took her as my wife," I explained. "Jadwiga has a gift. She cannot bear children but can help others conceive. She desperately wants to become a mother."

We all glanced at the potion that had now turned red. Jadwiga shut her eyes, still not aware of Mokosh's presence. White smoke filled the room once again, spreading faster than before.

"Can you see it?" Mokosh asked. "The witch has spectacular vision, Veles."

Mokosh tilted her head to the side and Jadwiga opened her eyes, lobbing her gaze from me to Mokosh.

"You have the ember of life within you. I can sense it," the goddess said in surprise.

Mokosh was dressed in brown leather pants and a black top that revealed her enormous breasts, her ebony hair flowing down her back.

"Who are you and what do you know about my gift?"

Jadwiga asked in an exhausted tone. This potion was proving to be challenging and she needed all the strength she could get.

"I can sense the ember of life within you. It's been passed on to you from your mother," Mokosh explained.

"Can you take it away?"

"You can't fix the unfixable—your gift is special. It creates life in the womb, so it's a great blessing," Mokosh explained, sounding melancholic.

Jadwiga swallowed hard and stared at her for a long moment. Mokosh was right—she couldn't change her. This would go against nature and all the laws that had been written in the past.

We couldn't fix Jadwiga—her only chance was the potion. I caught the disappointment in her eyes and sensed her overwhelming sadness.

"I cannot heal myself. You must take away this gift," Jadwiga insisted, approaching her and quickly grabbing her hands.

"But this gift is such a blessing to others. You're a special witch Yaga," Mokosh added, looking away before she continued. "It could only mean one thing."

"What does it mean? And why do I have it?" Yaga asked. She still labelled it as a curse, but was it really?

"It means that your power hasn't developed yet. I think you might be part goddess. If there is the ember of life within you, then this can also mean that someone in your family line was visited by a god or goddess in the past," she said. "I know what you want, but I cannot help you. I cannot heal something that's already healed."

Mokosh was right, but this statement was confusing for Jadwiga. She must have realised that fixing her wasn't possible. Her grandmother must have had the ember of life within her and the gift only manifested in Jadwiga. Her mother had died when she was young and Jadwiga didn't know anything about her.

"This is impossible," Yaga whispered.

"You have so much power and potential. You are destined to lead the masses and maybe that's why you could help Veles conquer his brother. That's why he is here and why he married you."

The potion continued to boil and still required Jadwiga's attention.

Yaga sighed, then brushed her hair away from her face, tired and defeated.

Despite her power and ambition, she wasn't ready to break her curse. All the ingredients melted together inside the mortar, but darkness hovered on the surface, trying to break through. At some point, Jadwiga would have to drink it—but not until it was ready.

CHAPTER 6
JADWIGA

"**I** know I can get pregnant and there must be someone who can help take away my gift. For now this potion is my only solution and I have to drink it once it settles," I said, addressing both Veles and his new companion. I couldn't believe the goddess of fertility was standing right in front of me and she wouldn't fix this problem for me.

I returned my attention to the brown liquid. Everything was going according to plan.

Veles was staring at me and I wasn't sure if I was supposed to say anything else.

"All right, I will leave you two lovebirds alone now. I am sorry I can't assist you but this is beyond my scope of expertise," the goddess explained before vanishing into thin air. Nothing was going to surprise me anymore, but she was not how I imagined her to be in the first place. In all the books I had read she was calm and feminine looking, but in reality she seemed … kinky.

I had to concentrate on this potion. The worst part of the spell was over. Now I just needed to wait until it was done. I felt

Veles' gaze on me and sweat gathered on my forehead. I could still feel the warmth of his lips on mine.

The kiss couldn't happen again. I had to forget about the fact that the tall and handsome god was staring at me with need and wouldn't leave me alone, even for a moment.

The desire I felt for him wasn't relevant. I couldn't get distracted and miss anything, after all the months of preparations. For the first time in a long while though, he made me feel warm and happy deep inside. I liked the way his hair fell on his shoulder, and when he kissed me I knew that I could lose my mind for him.

He was magnificent, yet the way he treated me like his possession annoyed me. Still, there was no point in denying that I wanted to taste what was forbidden.

"I'm being called somewhere, dear Yaga, so I must leave you. The whole manor is at your disposal. The dwarves will prepare food for you soon. When I return later, we will have dinner together," he announced, hesitant.

This place must be filled with other magical creatures. I frowned slightly, astonished that he was leaving me alone.

The smell emanating from the potions was horrendous. It would be a challenge to consume this beverage but I had to if I wanted a child. This was part of the process.

"Don't worry. I will read a few books to keep my mind occupied. See you in a few hours," I said, smiling.

He seemed satisfied with my answer and before I could ask another question, he was gone. Disappeared, just like Mokosh.

The whole place seemed empty without him. I was left with my thoughts and emotions. Using my wand, I magicked a glass of water.

After drinking, I got up and started walking around, running my hand over the titles sitting on the bookshelves along one wall.

This library was old, and some of the books were rare. Veles had thought of everything.

I had to keep an eye on the potion. The magic was fast rising, acquiring the essence of immortality. My family was probably worried about me, but Veles assured me that no one would remember a thing. Time must work differently here.

I wondered what had happened to Eric. Although our marriage was never intended to be about love, he'd been useful at times and I was concerned about him. Veles was planning something. He kept telling me that he wanted to get rid of his brother, but how did I factor into this?

I had been teaching at the Magic Academy of Lviv for over fifteen years now. This country was my home and the city was my soul.

Everyone who'd met me knew of my ambition, but not about my hidden nature.

I knew the consequences of my dabbling with dark magic: I would lose my magic and my freedom. The current chancellor was closed-minded and did everything by the book.

I hadn't killed anyone personally, but I'd hurt witchlords and witches. I wasn't proud of this, but it was the sacrifice I'd made in order to achieve my goal.

I picked up a book I thought would be interesting and started reading. Soon, I was immersed in the story and lost to the world outside. The potion was bubbling away while I kept turning the pages.

Around two hours later, I stretched in my seat, feeling a little tired and hungry. I figured Veles wasn't going to show up soon and I wanted to explore the manor house.

I was looking forward to dinner with him later. Gods stayed away from the mortal realm, but I'd heard rumours. Apparently, a few witchlords claimed a few sightings.

But humans had no idea about the existence of magic on

Earth, and the fact that witches, witchlords, and other creatures lived amongst them. For centuries, they were too preoccupied with their own affairs to notice or care about us.

After making sure I could leave the potion unattended for a few minutes, I left the room. There was still so much I had to learn, but I was on the right track to achieve immortality, especially after making a deal with the god of the underworld.

The manor was a little cold as I walked through the long corridors. Crossing through to the other side, I decided to get some fresh air, using the kitchen backdoor. I needed to decompress. It was already dark when I stepped outside. The stillness of the forest and the soft breeze welcomed me, imbuing me with positive energy.

I closed my eyes and took a deep breath as an unexplained pull drew me to the forest. I walked for several minutes, conscious that I couldn't wander too far.

Suddenly, a vision hit me. I saw myself standing in the old cottage with the low ceiling. A fire crackled in the huge fireplace in the middle of the room. This place was so cosy and warm. It felt like home. My books were on a table and I spotted a few of my flasks on the windowsill amongst the odd plants.

"I'm ready, Yaga."

The faint voice startled me. I looked to my right, seeing a soul drifting above the floor. A real ghost of a woman who'd passed as an elder. I knew her to be a witch.

"What do you want from me?" I asked her, baffled.

A heavy object then landed in my hands—a shiny black skull. The fire burning inside made it appear alive. My heartbeat accelerated.

I was the rightful owner of the firelight.

The sort of light that allowed me to open the gate to the underworld.

Now, everything slowly started to make sense. The old witch

had died and needed to pass to the other side. I swallowed hard, staring at the skull, mesmerised by its power.

"You must open the gate. You stole the firelight from Veles, so you're in charge of the gate now," she said.

Right after she spoke, I felt like I was being pulled away from this vision. I was back in a field and only then did I realise I'd walked deep into the forest. The manor was still visible in the distance but it would be too risky to keep going. Veles wouldn't be happy if he came back to find me gone.

I quickly turned around to retrace my steps, thinking about the vision and the firelight and what it all meant. Was I in charge of the world of the dead? The woman said I'd stolen it from Veles, but I couldn't have because he never even mentioned it to me.

"And where do you think you're going?"

A deep voice startled me out of nowhere and I abruptly swivelled on my feet. Then, thunder tore through the sky and I jumped, darting my gaze around to see who'd just spoken.

The air turned hot and clammy. Mist rose, swirling around my ankles, soon covering the ground and forest. Every hair on the back of my neck stood on end. A split second later, a witchlord appeared in front of me.

"For Perun," I cursed, losing my balance and landing on the grass.

His skin looked almost translucent in the gloom. Shirtless and broad-shouldered, his broad, hairy chest tapered over a ripped stomach, his muscles taut. Gorgeous.

The god stared deep into my eyes, not moving an inch. He smiled behind a dark beard while holding something in his right hand—a long stick that from my vantage point appeared to be a wand, but I wasn't sure.

My gaze trailed downwards over his form. With a sharp intake of breath, I noted the thick, dark hairs sticking out of his leather trousers, which sat low on his hips. A sudden wave of fear cut through my magic, seeping into my skin.

Why was he here? *Who* was he?

Rain fell harder now, although the trees were shielding us a little, and it didn't seem as though this ... being ... was getting soaked.

"A beautiful mortal female alone in the forest. I think today is my lucky day," he finally spoke, and I quickly shifted my eyes to his face. He was handsome, but much warmer looking than Veles. His features were sharp and defined. His eyes were a stormy brown with ether beneath his irises.

I knew in that moment that he was a god and I was lost. I had to get back to Veles.

No one was supposed to know about me and yet here this being was.

"Who are you and what are you doing in this place?" I asked. A tiny voice inside my head advised me to get up and run. I tried to stand but he pushed me back onto the grass.

"Not so fast, beautiful. I don't step into the mortal world often, but I'm always in need of fulfilling your deepest desires," he growled.

Adrenaline rushed from my veins when he grabbed my leg and pulled me closer to him. With a tight grip, he dragged me over the grass. He was surprisingly strong.

"I belong to another god," I shouted, and quickly started chanting spells, hoping my magic could distract him, but I didn't think it was affecting him. "What do you want from me?"

"I need you to tell me the location of the firelight," he said. "My name is Chernobog. I was sent here by Perun and I need you to give me access to Veles' magic."

I frowned because I didn't understand what he was saying. The soul from the vision had talked about firelight, too. This was very odd.

"Firelight. I have never heard of such a thing. What is it?" I asked. There had to be a connection between this and the vision I'd just had.

Chernobog tilted his head to the side, his fiery gaze betraying a primal desire to take and possess.

I wasn't afraid of Veles. For sure he was intimidating and powerful, but he didn't strike terror within me. But this god was something else. I wasn't sure what to expect or what he wanted from me.

My pulse started pounding in my ears and I struggled to breathe, trying to release my energy and magic, but his presence overwhelmed me.

I was away from home and my abilities were suppressed, so I had to pray for a real miracle.

CHAPTER 7
VELES

My time on the earth was slowly running out. I had no doubt that Jadwiga was powerful and she could help me defeat my brother, but there was still so much we needed to learn about each other.

If she was capable of creating dark magic, she was also capable of killing a god. Her magic was strong yet unpredictable, so I left her alone with her deadly potion so I could figure out the next step without distraction. Her presence could be … suffocating.

She desperately wanted to have a child and believed this potion was the answer to all her problems. But even I wasn't sure where I stood when it came to fulfilling her desire.

Mokosh whispered to me that I shouldn't get attached in case I had to go ahead and kill her, as per my original plan. This woman wasn't like other mortals. Although she could be replaced, I couldn't imagine being with someone else.

I had chosen this house because it was isolated and untraceable. A powerful witchlord had lived here before and this place was bound with magic that mortals or even witches wouldn't be able to break. Besides, I saw myself in the future with her here, in this exact place.

I intended to see Svarog again. He was much more knowledgeable than me in every aspect of human life. I gave him the firelight to take care of the souls—he was supposed to be the one leading them from the mortal realm all the way to Nawia while I was absent. He also wanted to see Perun defeated, but there were many challenges ahead.

Of the creatures that lived in this house, some remained loyal to their previous master, but others came out to serve me willingly. In their eyes, I was their new master and they were useful when I needed someone to keep an eye on my Jadwiga.

I still wielded great power over most of the gods, which made them envious of me. Some were waiting for me to slip so they could replace me. I had to be like my brother, untouchable and apparently indestructible. But only then would they respect me.

Little did they know he wasn't perfect.

Perun was aware that I was here in Slovenia, but he had no idea that Jadwiga even existed. He had never been interested in human affairs and this in itself was his greatest weakness.

In his infinite arrogance, Perun believed that he would rule forever, but he never should have underestimated me. And when he schemed to get rid of me, that was the last straw.

Jadwiga was my only way out. Her unique magic would become my weapon. But getting romantically involved would only complicate things. We'd lost control around each other, so I had to walk away.

I took a deep breath and closed my eyes for a moment. After I left her, I went to one of the bedrooms upstairs and entered another realm. Soon, everything started to vanish, the energy vibrated, and all material things disappeared.

She was safe in the house on her own. Mokosh would probably visit her again at some point; I sensed her nearby and trusted her for she still yielded to my authority.

"You've arrived much sooner than expected," the deep familiar voice said.

I smiled to myself. This beautiful realm was Svarog's finest creation. The sun shone brightly over a magnificent field, the ground carpeted with exquisitely hued flowers. A herd of deer were nibbling on the grass nearby.

Svarog approached as usual without his shirt on. The wind ruffled his blond hair.

I would rather have stayed with Jadwiga, but I couldn't yet deal with the feelings she woke in me. Depending on another was not something I was comfortable with. Yet, she somehow felt right. Familiar.

Many had warned me that I could start developing human feelings if I stayed in the mortal realm too long. I had a feeling they were right. Humanity affected me more than I realised and it was only the beginning.

"I ignored the calling for as long as I could, but this mortal is useful. We both know we need her. She's powerful, but I'm still unsure how she could help me defeat my brother," I replied. "It's her magic and her special gift that is the key to our security," I thought out loud. Jadwiga could help me destroy the god of thunder and give me the power to finally become ruler of all the realms.

Svarog didn't have an answer to my questions, but I yearned to come up with a different solution than crushing her spirit. Hurting and destroying her. There had to be another way. Svarog smiled as though he understood why I was so conflicted. He tilted his head to the side and released a deep breath.

"Let me take you to Zara, the water nymph. She should show you your future and then you will have your answers," he replied.

He was right. I needed to figure out if I was on the right path. Besides, Svarog had spent a lot of time on Earth. He lived a dual life. He'd experienced love, hardship, sadness and anguish, too. He understood everything whereas I had no idea what to expect.

I clearly needed guidance, but I was sceptical of the water nymphs.

"I'm not sure if this is such a good idea. The water nymphs cannot be trusted, brother. They are wild and tend to lie," I said, remembering what harm these territorial creatures had done to many in the mortal realm in order to protect themselves.

"Well you haven't met Zara yet. She's different and not like the others. She will show you what you need to know," he said defensively.

Svarog started to walk away from me. I shook my head and took a few deep breaths, telling myself that I had accepted this help from Svarog. So I followed him through the bucolic scenery, surrounded by flowers and buzzing insects. Wild animals grazed nearby.

This realm now belonged to the goddess of love and abundance but Svarog had added his touch to it, making it what it was today. I wished I could have visited more often. In the past century, I had been stuck in Nawia, juggling and condemning souls and being the rightful owner of the firelight.

Soon, my brother brought me to a lake where butterflies fluttered around, chasing each other. I was filled with calm and I had a feeling that this was Svarog's intention. The sun warmed my skin and I wondered if Jadwiga would like this place, too.

I breathed in the fresh air, pushing these thoughts away.

"Let's wait and see. She should be here soon," Svarog muttered.

The clear water started to bubble. Something was definitely approaching us. Not long after, the water nymph appeared above the surface. She was green, naked, and gorgeous with shimmering skin. Her turquoise eyes shone with bright powerful energy. She had little scales on her hands and arms. I ran my eyes over her body, admiring her perky breasts and wide hips.

"For Perun, what a pleasant surprise to see you both here, Gods. I must say I wasn't expecting the two of you," she said, her voice smooth and seductive.

I fast began to understand the appeal and why my brother was constantly hanging around these creatures. The nymphs were pleasing to the eye and were probably exceptional lovers, too.

Svarog liked the company of beautiful demons and since his fire was useful, he used it as a trade—also because he enjoyed playing with mortal creatures. The trade was fair because nymphs used it to supplement their own magic.

"Hello, Zara. This is my brother, Veles. He's the god of the underworld and he comes with a question for you," Svarog greeted.

I stood on the banks of the lake, watching as the nymph swam hesitantly towards me. Maybe she didn't want to believe I was truly the god that resided in Nawia.

She emerged from the water, levitating over the surface. Magic rose to the fore, heavy and intense. She was stunning, curvy in all the right places, and her perfectly rounded breasts were begging for attention. Her pubic area was covered by a large leaf and long, dark hair flowed down her back and arms. Svarog growled next to me. I could sense his desire for this creature.

In that moment, I pictured myself with Jadwiga, her spread on the bed naked while I pleasured her. These thoughts were haunting me now and I hadn't even tasted her yet. Blood rushed to my groin, spreading down to my cock.

This fire within me burned so brightly, it was driving me to insanity. I wondered when this anguish was going to end.

"Well, well, well. The god of the underworld is gracing me with his presence." The water nymph giggled.

"Show me how I can use this human to destroy my brother, Perun," I demanded, impatience taking a bite at me—one of my acquired human traits.

The nymph moved her hands and the water bubbled, then smoke began to rise. Such ancient magic used to belong to elves.

The landscape started to change. The sky went dark and gloomy with a storm approaching. The sun hid behind heavy clouds.

The surface of the water then showed me images of a possible future. Jadwiga stood with another mortal or witchlord. He was much younger but I could tell he was important to her. I stepped closer, hoping the nymph would show me more.

The scene changed and now, Jadwiga stood on a platform facing a crowd. This was another timeline because she looked much older.

"This woman desires immortality and she's going to trick you," the nymph said.

"Show me more. I need to see the mortal she's with again," I demanded, feeling tense and aggravated that the images had changed so fast. The nymph nodded, giggling again and sending flirtatious looks to Svarog.

The mortal appeared in the vision again. Dark-haired, he wore a dark cloak and looked familiar.

"You must give this witch a child. That's what she wants, but you must be careful because she's devious and deceitful. She won't give you what you need, and you'll be locked in Nawia forever," the nymph warned.

"How could the child help me destroy my brother forever?" I asked, staring down at the water and wishing I could make heads or tails of this vision.

Jadwiga seemed happy and proud. Then she glanced at her

witchlord companion and smiled warmly. The crowd started to cheer; everyone was screaming her name, and the magic spread everywhere. Witches flew above the crowd, creating explosions of magic. Even as an older woman, Jadwiga remained beautiful. I didn't understand why I wasn't there with her and why she wasn't immortal. Did she manage to replace me already? This didn't feel right.

"Yes, the child is the key. If you impregnate her, then you will be more powerful than Perun. You will be the god above all gods, and you will rule forever," she said before adding, "On the other hand, you could kill her. Her death could also give you what you need. Not many know that if you take someone's soul, you will be more powerful than you can imagine, but that's too dangerous. It will lead you to another path, one you don't want to go to. So there's either death or love."

"So you're telling me that if I give her a child then she will love me, and I would be able to stay with her?" I asked for clarification.

"Staying with her isn't necessary for you. I don't see you beside her and if you choose to do that then she will weaken you for you'd become more human. You won't die, but you will age right with her. Also, beware, the mortal witch isn't sure if she can trust you yet."

"This is good news, brother. You have to seduce Yaga and show her you care; otherwise your plan won't work," my brother interfered.

I didn't think he realised that this wasn't such wonderful news, because I still had to make a decision.

I took a deep breath and dragged my hands through my long brown hair. This realm was slowly falling apart, as would some realms that existed purely per a god's request. This was a sign I needed to leave right away. My skin was burning with desire for Yaga. Would this be the end of her ... or me?

Maybe there was a way for me to change this law that gods couldn't give life. I wasn't sure who made the rules in that respect. I had to try to fulfil my promise to her because this was the only way for me to conquer my brother—the only way I was prepared to entertain. Everybody would forget about him and my power would prevail.

"Thank you for your service and the visions. I think it's time for me to go," I said.

The nymph giggled, then the images of Jadwiga and other man disappeared. I remained confused, but felt compelled to make a leap of faith. Diving into the water, she could be seen no more.

"I will come and visit soon to see how the things are progressing between you two," my brother said, giving me the side eye that I knew so well. He was more hopeful than me.

"Looking forward to that. Now I must leave. I have to speak to her right away."

I returned to the same spot where I showed up in this realm. The darkness was descending and the magic was vanishing. I shut my eyes and took a few deep breaths. When I opened them, I was back in the old manor house, in the same bedroom I'd used to enter the other realm.

My skin prickled with the awareness of her lingering scent. Something felt off because the house seemed empty.

I rushed downstairs, certain she hadn't just gone and left the building. When I entered the room I'd left her in, I found it full of white smoke.

The potion was bubbling, releasing more darkness, and I couldn't fathom why Jadwiga wasn't tending to it. She was nowhere to be seen and I found myself unable to sense her anywhere nearby.

She had either escaped or was taken from me.

CHAPTER 8
JADWIGA

I was no longer in the manor or the forest. He'd taken me somewhere else—to an underground party at another estate and possibly, in another country. Gods moved beyond space and time. I saw humans, witches, witchlords and many other creatures from all over Opana gathering in the crowded place.

The sight fascinated me. I couldn't leave the potion for too long though. I had to return and continue with the magic.

"What do you want from me? I don't know anything about the firelight and I must go back to the manor house. The god of the underworld will be searching for me, and I have important things to see to." Energy sparked off my finger. Chernobog was dangerous. He must have realised I was Veles' property and that was why he kidnapped me.

I should have never left the manor. Now I only had an hour or two before the potion would get spoiled. Veles had no idea how to complete it. And there was only one chance to get it right —if missed, it would be ruined forever.

This god was tall and well-built. He reminded me of an

ancient warrior. He held my hand and scanned the crowd.

"You won't be going anywhere, my dear witch. I want you to stay here and enjoy yourself. This is your punishment for being with Veles and you're my property now. He doesn't deserve you," the god replied, smiling.

Stunned, I frowned, but when I opened my mouth to ask him about Veles, he pushed me into the throng of people. Then, when I looked up, Chernobog was gone. This party was going in full swing. People danced around, getting into my space. I cursed and started chanting spells, but my magic was silent. This wasn't a great sign.

Chernobog was nowhere to be seen and I wondered why he left me here on my own.

I needed to find a way out, but after a while I noticed that most of the people at the party were either naked or didn't wear many clothes at all. Men and women were kissing and fucking each other right in front of everyone else.

Yes, I wasn't seeing things. This was happening for real and I quickly figured out I was witnessing an orgy.

Suddenly, my magic rushed to the surface of my skin, igniting a fire inside me, but it was only for a moment because it suddenly died out again. I had no time to dally. I had to get back, but I was useless without my magic or my wand, which I must have left in the manor or lost somewhere when Chernobog took me.

I started to manoeuvre my way among the naked, sweaty people, hoping to find a way out and get back to Veles. Chernobog couldn't keep me prisoner in this hellhole. If there was a way in, there had to be an exit.

I spotted two couples by the pillars getting it on and froze, unable to look away. One woman, a human, was on her knees, sucking a witchlord's cock. I wondered what a human was doing in here.

All I could hear around me were loud moans and heavy breathing. The energy and scent of sex were vibrant and powerful.

A table at the back was laden with selections of wine and finger foods that I didn't dare touch. I looked around, hoping to stand on something to see if this room was big enough or to figure out the location of the exit doors, but I couldn't see any stools or chairs.

The hairs on my arms stood on end when I spotted three men walking towards me through the crowd of naked bodies. They were no doubt magical, but they couldn't have been just ordinary witchlords—they seemed much more powerful. They clearly got my attention. The one to my right with black hair and swarthy skin was dressed in black armour. He was like a moving shadow with his penetrating brown eyes, scanning his surroundings. The other wore white armour and possessed fair skin, blond hair, and clear blue eyes.

The third was dressed in red. The contrast between them was significant and I couldn't take my eyes off them. They all looked like warriors or soldiers from Opana's army.

"You appear to be lost, my lady," the dark one said as they all stopped right in front of me.

No one was paying much attention to them and I had no clue why they'd singled me out, but they probably knew how to get the hell out of this party.

"I need to get out. I was kidnapped by a god called Chernobog and brought here. I'm a witch and I must urgently return to a house in Slovenia to tend to an important matter," I told them.

"My name is Constantine and this is Andrei. That's our third brother, Vlad. We are riders who serve powerful entities and are searching for our next master. I can sense you have been in the presence of a god," he said.

For some odd reason, I felt like these men were important—as though they'd be instrumental in my future.

"Yes, I have, but I am trapped here and I need to find my way out," I insisted.

Veles wouldn't know what to do to save the potion. Besides, he wasn't connected to the spell the way I was. I was the only one who could finish brewing the Flask of Nightmares.

"Can you take us to him? We arrived in this realm seeking an opportunity to serve a god," the blond called Andrei said.

Their magic was strong, drifting around and making its presence known.

"We could help each other. Get me out of here and I'll make sure you have your audience with the god of the underworld. He resides in Nawia," I said, proposing a deal. I needed my wand for self-defence. Without it, I was weaker.

All the riders exchanged looks when a naked woman approached, moving seductively. She caressed Andrei's armour and whispered in his ear, then said in a loud voice, "Hello, stranger. Do you want to play with me? I'm so wet…"

I suddenly became very self-conscious, wishing I could just disappear.

The other riders watched her with open curiosity when she turned and licked Costa's ear. He stood motionless, as if oblivious to her affections.

"No, my lady, not right now. As you can see, we are occupied, but I will find you later once I finish my business here," he replied.

"Don't go too far," Andrei added, grinning.

I was fascinated by all of them, especially by the third one who was now staring at me. He had long, unkempt grey hair bound in a messy ponytail. His burning gaze elevated my energy. For a moment I thought he was trying to read my thoughts.

"Find a man in a blue cloak. He will take you to the exit

doors. This whole place has been charmed. We cannot lead you outside but we could help you leave this realm once the witchlord in a blue cloak helps you to break the wards that bind you to this space," the black rider explained.

The woman finally walked away and I was glad for that, but just then, the couple that was fucking by one of the pillars started making moaning sounds.

The woman screamed out her orgasm, her hands tangled in the man's hair. I hoped to find an exit soon because this place was decadent and addictive, making me hot and bothered.

Sweat gathered on the side of my brow. I pushed these unexpectedly erotic thoughts away to focus on my task, but that was rather difficult when everyone around me was fucking each other. All I could hear were moans and panting.

"So there is a man or witchlord who could assist me?" I asked to clarify.

"Yes, he knows us and if you tell him we sent you, he will help you break the wards. The gods' magic is strong and we are bound to our duties. We cannot go against a god," the dark one explained.

The riders served the higher entities so they couldn't interfere —I understood that.

"All right, I will do that and if everything works out then you have my word. I will take you to Veles. It's a deal," I said, then reached out to shake Constantine's hand.

After it was all said and done, the three riders backed away from me, vanishing in the crowd.

I figured that spotting a man in a blue cloak wouldn't be too challenging because everyone here was either naked or wearing minimal clothes. But time wasn't on my side and the fact that my magic remained silent made me a little worried. I pushed through the crowd, passing two women and a man in a corner.

The man was fucking her from behind while the other woman was rubbing her nipples.

My throat went dry as I felt the vibrating energy of desire deep in the pit of my stomach. I had to pull myself together. I had to ignore the extreme arousal I felt in this moment. It was just another distraction that kept me away from my goal.

This orgy was only happening in my imagination—all these people fucking each other weren't really here. I negotiated my way, feeling more frustrated with every step. Then, all of a sudden, someone grabbed me.

"Hello, beautiful witch. I have been told you need to be taken care of. Let me taste you," the stranger said.

He moved his giant hands over my waist and brought me flush to his body. I tried to push him but I was so overwhelmed and aroused I just let him touch me. The overwhelming urge to be close to someone was something I couldn't shake. His body felt so warm and good. Right then, the man in the blue cloak wasn't important anymore.

Then he grabbed my cheeks and held me while we stared into each other's eyes. I'd never seen anyone so beautiful and handsome.

"Yes, take me away from here," I cooed. I didn't even want to say those words, but something made me. Then another voice whispered that he was going to help me and I needed to go with him.

The Flask of Nightmares, Veles and the riders, all these people and things weren't important to me anymore. I just had to satisfy my craving for a man's touch. I wanted him to make love to me. He promised that he was going to fuck me hard.

He led me away from the room until everything was dark and I found myself drifting into the unknown. When I came around, I was sitting on the bed and my hands were tied up behind me. Something was very wrong and I suddenly remembered that I was supposed to find the man in a blue cloak.

Then I also realised I was naked. My nipples were hard and my legs were spread wide. The man stood in front of me, right by the bed—so stunning. His skin shimmered and his blond hair fell on his shoulders—another god that came to claim me. Everything was so confusing, but I was throbbing for him, and I could barely stand the fire blazing within me.

"It's better if we have privacy. I've listened to your thoughts and know what you were looking for. I can satisfy you, my dear," he said, pushing a whip he held in his hand between my legs. I shuddered breathing hard and thinking that I was supposed to be somewhere else. This didn't feel right.

"Please, just let me go; I shouldn't be here. I have to find a man in a blue cloak so he can lead me out of this realm," I pleaded, attempting to no avail to activate my magic. My skin was normally static with electric current, but not here. Besides, I didn't have my wand.

The man or god smiled, moved around the bed and sat beside me. When he touched my arm with his large hands, I gasped. Then he caressed my hip, back up to between my breasts. His touch was like fire on my skin. I shut my eyes to control this fiery arousal that overwhelmed me.

"Not yet, my dear. First, I have to give you pleasure," he said, his gaze roaming over my naked body.

Before I could say a word, he produced a shiny blade and cut the skin on my stomach, making me scream. I shook my head, shouting at him to stop. Dull pain shattered through me and blood poured out of the wound, staining the white sheets.

"I had to mark you for Chernobog, so no one else will ever touch you. Now let's see how wet you are for me," he said before dipping a finger inside me.

I cried out, this time in pleasure. I wanted him to do so

much more, to fill me up with his huge cock. But something was holding me back. The tiny voice in the back of my mind kept whispering that I didn't truly want this.

My mind was clear. And I was calling out for my magic over and over, attempting to remove the blocks. This god had to have used his power to keep me confined and secluded.

"You're so wet for me and your pussy craves my cock. Let's play one of my favourite games. Let's see how long it takes you to beg me to make you come," he said, moving behind me.

I couldn't see him for I was restrained and he wouldn't let me turn. My legs were spread and when I tried to close them, some sort of spell kept me immobile. My magic refused to come to my aid. I had never felt more afraid in my life.

He finally came into view, naked, his massive cock standing at half-mast. I stared at him in horror.

Deep down I knew I didn't want this. He'd spirited me away from the crowd and the riders. Yet, unexplained arousal muddled my thinking.

I started to pant for air, shaking my head and chanting spells as he caressed my breasts.

"No… get away from me. Please, I don't want this," I pleaded, but he only laughed and pinched my clit, easing two fingers inside me while I cried out, ready to orgasm. I shut my eyes, telling myself that this was just a nightmare, that he was projecting this illusion on me.

"Oh, but you're so wet and I can smell your desire, woman," he said. "I won't let you go anywhere else because you're mine for a night. So let's see how fast you can come for me."

He leaned down to my breasts and started licking them furiously. I shrieked, cursing at him and demanding he stop when suddenly, the door opened and someone barged inside.

"You're touching what's mine and for that, I reduce you to ash, God."

CHAPTER 9
VELES

Jadwiga wasn't in the manor and possibly not even in this realm. I had to act fast and figure out what to do next. Some god must be up to no good and taken her.

No one apart from Mokosh and Svarog knew about this place—no human, witch, or witchlord. Yet, someone had betrayed me.

This realm coexisted with the others that were purposely created to serve the gods. Svarog had shaped the one where the water nymph resided, but he was loyal. Mokosh too hated Perun and she wouldn't have risked Jadwiga's life.

This was filling me with unease. My senses were on full alert even while still sensing her. Smelling her. She must have only just vanished. I finally tracked her scent to the kitchen and then to the door that led outside.

In moments, I was stepping into someone's residence in another realm. It was a crowded orgy involving many naked men and women. I glanced around, registering only positive emotions. I knew right away that this orgy was a god's creation.

Normally, this was Svarog's speciality but I had no doubt he wasn't the one that took Yaga.

Whoever it was would be reduced to ash because he dared to touch what was mine. I couldn't take this kind of disrespect. I knew for a fact that if anyone was so crazy to ever cross Perun, the consequences would be severe. Others feared him, including the gods. That was another reason why I was so desperate to take away his power, to destroy him once and for all.

Perun would kill everyone who stood in his way. I wanted others to bow to me and fear me as they did my brother. The fact he threatened my position only made me act faster.

I glanced around the room, seeing many witches and human females consorting with men, witchlords, and gods. The latter were in disguise but they didn't fool me.

The room vibrated with strong sexual tension. This whole thing felt overwhelming and daunting. Normally I wasn't affected by it, but now I was filled with unease because I was worried about my wife.

I moved around the room, amid flushed faces and keening moans, searching.

Jadwiga's scent was still fresh and I imagined being here with her, exploring her body and making her scream for more. I was no longer interested in any other women, no matter how beautiful or magical. There was only one I craved. This should have shocked me, but in that moment, it hit home.

The energy shifted, expanding and rippling. I kept going, observing the sex, the exchanges in energy vibrations and the hard fucking that was going on almost everywhere. A few of the women were screaming in pain, begging their partners to stop. At last, I spotted Chernobog by one of the pillars. I should have known it had been him who entered the manor in my absence.

My brother was fucking a beautiful red-headed woman that was chained up to the wall with a red mask on. He was panting like crazy and their energy was filled with sexual dominance. She begged him to stop, releasing sounds of both pleasure and pain.

I stood there for a moment wondering how he'd found out about my Jadwiga. Chernobog was irrelevant, but he sometimes wandered off to a few of my realms, looking for adventures.

I then marched to him and grabbed him, pulling him out of the woman. Anger rushed through my veins and I was ready to break his neck.

"You need time off, brother. We have unfinished business to discuss," I growled, slamming him against the wall.

His face was all red and his eyes were glossed over, lost in the throes of orgasmic frenzy. I quickly released the woman from her chains and barked at her to leave us. Nodding frantically, she vanished from sight.

A few people had noticed this exchange, but they weren't going to interfere because they knew what would happen to them if they did. Chernobog was off the chain during these orgies, but tonight he was high on ambrosia and other potions. It was time to teach him a lesson—one he would never forget.

"Where the fuck is my woman?" I roared, wanting to suffocate him, but this death would have been too easy. He needed to suffer.

"Brother, there are plenty of women here. Just pick one," he croaked out, madness in his eyes.

"You came here with a witch you took from my realm. What happened to her?"

He was panting for air, staring at me in confusion. I knew it was going to take him some time to get out of that erotic frenzy. The truth was that I wanted to kill him, reduce him to ash, but it was never easy to destroy a god.

I would have to take him back to Nawia and then make him remember the fiery pits over and over again. Maybe then he would finally understand that he couldn't fuck with what was mine.

"There's plenty of other witches here… just pick one, brother," he repeated. "I don't recall that any of them ever belonged to you," he rasped as I held him above the ground, but he was too intoxicated with ambrosia and magic to feel anything. I was slowly beginning to lose patience, so I pulled out a blade that I liked using sometimes. Then I brought it to his neck, against his sweaty skin.

"You took a powerful and beautiful mortal witch. She is mine. She told you she belonged to me and you still brought her here. The consequences of your actions are going to be very severe, brother, so tell me … where is she? What have you done to her?"

My breathing was laboured and I was ready to rip Chernobog to pieces because he still wasn't getting it. I removed the blade from his neck and placed it by his groin.

"She's probably being used," the god growled, so then I pushed the blade into his flesh right next to his balls. He roared in pain and his whole body shook in my tight grip.

Some woman screamed in ecstasy behind us.

I finally let go of him and he slid slowly down to the floor, cursing while he was badly bleeding. Unfortunately this wasn't going to kill him, but it pleased me that he was feeling pain.

It wasn't the same as human pain because their sensations were always heightened, but I made it intense enough for him to understand the level of my rage.

"One of my men must have taken her and he is probably playing with her upstairs. My magic wasn't working. That witch wasn't obedient, so I got bored," he spat, trying to lift himself up but he was too weak.

"Pray for Perun that she hasn't been harmed because I will make you suffer for it, brother," I warned him.

I was clearly developing human feelings and emotions towards Yaga. Being in this realm intensified these vibrations. Chernobog was much weaker than me, but he was still a God.

"You have no power over me brother. Everyone here knows that," he scoffed.

"I shall cut off your fat cock and feed it to one of your females, but time is of the essence and I must leave," I said, calmly.

I started walking away, shaking with fury as I tried to figure out where Jadwiga was being held. This place was like a maze and most rooms were occupied by all sorts of pairings. Threesomes, foursomes ... every position imaginable.

As time went on, panic settled in—paralysing.

But at last, her scent drifted to me, beckoning. I barged inside a room, taking the door out of its hinges. Sure enough, another entity lay on the bed, next to my wife. She was tied up, unable to move, and begging him to stop.

His fingers were inside her pussy and he was trying to bring her to the edge. Rage rippled through me as I stepped towards them.

"You're going to suffer for touching what's mine!" I growled, focusing my magic to make him rise up above the bed.

Jadwiga screamed. The magic was so potent and vibrant, aggravating me further.

His eyes popped out of his sockets he started shaking and spilling threats, saliva dripping down his chin. He clearly had no idea who I was. I was trying to focus, but this was becoming difficult because Jadwiga was on the bed naked.

She looked stunning, and that just added to my rage. In a flash, I made the entity explode to pieces. He shrieked in agony as his bones crumbled, so I crushed them, ripping his cells apart, so his body turned into one giant mass on the floor. Pieces of him scattered everywhere, covering the walls all around. The room looked like a tornado of blood and guts had gone through it.

He didn't exist in this realm anymore, no longer a problem.

Jadwiga was terrified, so I quickly freed her. She started sobbing loudly, but soon she wasn't going to remember any of it. I shut my eyes, grabbed her hand, and then we were leaving this realm.

Within moments, we were back in the manor house and she was sobbing in my arms. I tried to understand what was happening and why she felt this anguish and sorrow. Her emotions hit me like a brick wall. I felt every part of her being.

Her pain was so devastating, I couldn't bear it. I wanted to rip Chernobog to pieces for allowing the other god to lay his hands on her.

Jadwiga was covered in blood, so I had to clean her up. I had to find a way to take out that pain and anguish or I might lose my mind. All these emotions were tough to deal with. Back in Nawia I didn't need to feel things, but here I was too absorbed in her sensations to be able to push them away.

"What happened? My memories are foggy, Veles?" she asked when the crying ended.

I tried to think of a suitable answer, glad her memories of that place we just left were gone from her mind.

"You were taken from me. One of my brothers found you and transported you to an orgy in another realm. There, one of the gods tried to use you for his pleasure," I explained. "I arrived just in time before he could finish what he started."

I held her close, admiring her beautiful skin, her perky breasts and hardened pink nipples. Despite her ordeal, her pussy throbbed with need. That amazed me.

I hungered for her, aching to taste her, to sink my cock into her and mark her as mine, but I couldn't bring myself to touch her just yet. Yaga was in shock and I couldn't take advantage of her. When we lay together, I wanted her to enjoy the experience to the full.

"My thoughts are racing and some of my memories are missing."

"You have been through a lot, let me take you to the washroom in the basement first. You must wash away the blood and grime."

She didn't need to know that I'd only just created the basement with the old washroom-style room. She also didn't need to know what that god had done to her.

I could admire her naked body in my arms when she was coming apart. My mind was already picturing her on her knees with my cock in her mouth, but right now was not the time. Rest and recovery were needed.

"For Perun, what about my potion?" she suddenly asked. "How long have we been away?"

I put her down and fetched a cloak. Meanwhile, I had no doubt the potion was spoiled, beyond the point of salvaging.

"Jadwiga, I have something to share…" She looked up expectantly as I put the cloak on her shoulders and covered her. "It's been a few hours and I fear the potion is lost. But I had to come and save you … I'm so sorry." I should have done more to protect it, but I was blinded by worry and rage.

Her mouth gaped open and then she began to sob, hiding her face in her palms. Suddenly, I couldn't fucking breathe. My heart bled with sorrow.

I'd been so distraught, I forgot about her deepest wish: to have a child. Now, all was lost. The magic was spoiled and the process couldn't be reversed.

"You will get pregnant; I promise you that. I don't know how but I will find a way. Please, Yaga, don't be saddened by this news because my heart is breaking for you," I said.

Her eyes glistened with tears. I wasn't sure how I could

manage to create life, but I just made her a promise I had to fulfil.

She was supposed to be my weapon, the only living being that could destroy Perun, and yet at this juncture, I couldn't imagine hurting her.

I couldn't bring myself to even think about ending her life.

"I don't want to be like this, crying, but I've worked so hard to collect all the ingredients. I hope you killed that man who took me! I hope you made him suffer," she said with scorn.

"Trust me, no one crosses me and escapes my wrath. He is suffering," I stated. "Now let's get you all cleaned up."

Jadwiga probably smelled the blood. She looked down at her arms and legs and winced, seeing the pieces of skin and blood.

I took her to the basement. She gasped, looking around the beautiful washroom with large steamy pool in the middle. I created golden fountains and faucets for her. I made sure she had everything she needed in there but I didn't think I could just walk away now and leave her alone. I had to make sure that she was going to be all right.

Guilt wracked me. Although creating life would be going against nature for me and I'd be judged for that, I owed this to her. My brother Perun would allow something like this—he was known for bending the rules—but I was here because I wanted to end him. I could never ask for his help.

She looked around, lost in her thoughts for a moment.

"What about the fire magic? I'm sure this could give me what I need. The fire magic could create life," she asked.

She wrapped her cloak around her, shivering, so I lit all the torches on the walls to make it warm and cosy.

"We can discuss this another time. Right now you must wash up," I said. She had to get better.

"But there must be a way, right? Veles, you're incredibly powerful so you could make it happen," she insisted.

"Mokosh is the goddess of life. She must know how to change the laws," I said, finally giving in.

Her face brightened up and she smiled.

"Wonderful," she murmured. "I love this room so I'll bathe now."

She started to remove her cloak and I turned around, trying to respect her privacy. I was hard once again, aching to touch her, kiss and caress her all over … but I had to give her time.

"Where are you going, Veles?" she asked, her soft voice echoing in the room when I made to walk away.

I turned around to find her half immersed in the water. The energy was pulling us towards each other and I couldn't take my eyes off her. Even with the evidence of what just happened marking her body.

My gaze darted down to her pink areolas and wished I would take them in my mouth, one at a time. I wanted to dive between her legs and pleasure her until she screamed my name.

"I don't think I can stay," I admitted.

"Why?"

"Because I won't be able to control myself around you. I want to do unforgivable things to your body, to your soul, but we both know you have been through a lot," I said, inhaling sharply.

She smiled, then tossed her hair away from her face. "But I don't remember any of it, and now I'm here with you." She went deeper into the water. "Stay for a while. Watch me," she said softly.

CHAPTER 10
JADWIGA

My mind was still blank. I didn't remember much from the past several hours, but at this point I was too absorbed in Veles to care about my memories.

He was standing, watching me from a distance while I was immersed in water, naked and unbelievably aroused. Desire gleamed in his eyes, and his body didn't lie. He was rock-hard.

The water was warm and so relaxing. His magic was going haywire and I relished that. I wanted him to lose control. We had been playing the game of cat and mouse for too long now, and it was getting boring.

My magic stirred. I suddenly recalled standing outside the house talking to a god, then I was hit with flashbacks of my time in the other realm. An orgy. A sea of people engaged in all manner of depravity. I remembered encountering three riders, but after that, everything was foggy. I believed that my magic was helping me to remember that experience.

The riders were important. I didn't know why or how, but my intuition told me that they were going to be a part of my life even if this memory wasn't truly relevant right now.

Veles wanted to leave me here alone, but I couldn't let him go just yet. The cut on my stomach hurt, so I started to gently clean it while Veles regarded me with a softness and concern that tugged at my heartstrings.

I wanted him to make love to me. We were finally alone and … I needed him. No one would disturb us here.

Despite his caring attitude, I could sense his hunger as he travelled his gaze over my nakedness.

I stood up out of the water, smiling at him. Biting my bottom lip, I moved my hands down over my hips, making circles over my stomach where the cut was already healing, then farther down between my legs. I was so wet for him and ready to finally be seduced by this beautiful giant.

I wanted to drag my fingers through his chestnut hair as he sucked greedily on my nipples. He was truly a powerful being but with me he was more human than he realised. I was devastated by the fact that my precious potion was lost forever.

The Flask of Nightmares became my real-life nightmare and I was so disappointed. I'd put so much effort, done unforgivable things for nothing.

Firelight magic could take away my gift—this was my only option now. Veles blamed himself, but he had what I desired.

Right in that moment, we both had to forget about the past and focus on each other. He needed me to conquer his brother—one of the most powerful gods in the universe—and I needed him so I could become a mother.

"You are tempting me, woman, and this isn't good. I don't want to hurt you," he said in a husky voice.

I didn't answer. I was too turned on to even think about consequences. Dipping my finger inside my folds, I released a moan.

"Veles, I want you. Please touch me," I begged. Right then,

the flashbacks from the orgy became vivid. And I ached for him, more than ever.

"Get back into the water. You're testing me," he ordered.

I did as he asked.

Would he spank me? Punish me? This vision felt so real. For some reason I knew it had happened already. We were married and yet, we still hadn't consummated our relationship.

Veles needed to stop holding back. I kept circling my finger over my clit, trying to bring pleasure to myself. My breaths were shallow as I paced myself, yet he stood still. The warm, soothing water bubbled around me and the smell of jasmine wafted in the air, caressing my body. My nipples were hard, so I twisted my left breast, trailing my forefinger gently over the nipple.

"You're playing with fire, Yaga," he said, tilting his head to the side, watching me with fire in his eyes.

"And you're making this more difficult than it needs to be. Just get in," I said more firmly this time.

I was so aroused that I couldn't think straight. Veles needed to act upon his desire. His urges were human and raw, just like mine. Couldn't he see?

We both wanted this. On one side of the pool was a line of golden faucets with running water. I immersed myself deeper and started swimming across, full of anticipation.

The water felt wonderful when I finally made it to the faucets. The air was charged with tension. I was prepared for anything and was even willing to beg him to take me right then and there.

The dim light from the torches, the smell of burning wood and his addictive magic blended to feed my hunger for him.

I pushed my hips upwards, letting the water fall over my pussy. I burst out laughing, then whimpered with pleasure.

The water current hit the right spot, driving me closer to the edge. At this rate, I was going to come hard…

This position wasn't particularly comfortable and soon, my hips started to protest. Yet, I hated to move for it felt so good.

"Touch yourself. Show me how much you want to come, Jadwiga," came Veles' order then. Music to my ears.

I swallowed thickly and dipped my finger deep inside.

I held on. The water was still bouncing over that whole engorged area, making me lose my fucking mind. Soon, I was panting for breath, imagining his hands on me, teasing my clit.

With these visions in my head, I started fucking myself with my fingers and my body was set ablaze. I kept a steady rhythm, in and out, until an orgasm rocked through every part of my body, shattering me. I came apart, pleasure filling my cells, spreading everywhere, and I lost myself to the sensations.

Although masturbating was satisfying enough, the orgasm was underwhelming. But if Veles touched me, he would make me forget my name. His touch would be like melted lava on my skin.

When I finally opened my eyes, he stood in front of me at the edge of the water. His cock strained in his trousers and magic was softly caressing my nipples, then the rest of my body. He stared at me with such intensity, I thought I might come again.

"You have no idea how much I want to touch you right now," he growled.

"Then do it. What are you waiting for?" I urged.

"Fuck, Yaga. You have been hurt and need time to recover. I'm afraid I might hurt you." He huffed, dragging his hand through his hair.

I bit my bottom lip then fixed my gaze on his huge erection.

"In that case, I think it's my duty to take care of you now, Veles," I cooed. "Take off your pants, now don't you?"

He was lost in thought, hesitating, torn between desire and doing what was right. That made me want him more. When I was about to give up and get out of the water, he finally pulled his pants down. His cock sprang free after he took off his underpants. My eyes widened in shock and a gasp escaped my lips. I swallowed hard as I ran my gaze over his length.

I craved him more than I could comprehend. I needed him to touch me, fuck me … consume me.

"I don't think this will fit," I said, a little worried.

"Oh, my dear Yaga, it will, trust me. You can take it." He laughed as I stared at his huge cock trying to convince myself it would be all right, but with every passing second, I began to lose my newly-found confidence. I had never seen any man with such a sizeable manhood and I was certain he was going to bust me open with that thing.

Then I reminded myself that Veles was the god of the underworld, a supernatural being who could make me come like no other. He saved me from being raped by his own brother. He could do anything—including making sure I felt no pain.

Besides, the need to have him inside me overrode any fear or worry I might feel.

The torches cast a mysterious light on him. Veles stood in front of me in all his glory, while my sex continued to throb. My breathing quickened as he got on his knees and brought his length to inches from my face.

"Suck it, Yaga," he ordered, and the tip of his shaft brushed over my chin. I had a sudden desire to wipe some of my sweat on him.

"Veles," I breathed in, somehow now aware that we weren't alone in the manor. For some reason, this was turning me on even more. His heavy eyes were on me as the urge to taste him got stronger.

I wanted to please him so much but at the same time, I was a little afraid because of his size.

"Take it in your mouth and suck me before I lose control of myself," he growled.

His skin burned and tingled with energy. I did what he asked, took him in my mouth, then ran my lips over the tip. He groaned, watching my every move.

I cupped his balls and oh for Perun, he tasted divine, even when I was struggling to fit him in my mouth. His body tensed and he emitted a primitive sound in the back of his throat as I sucked harder. Fantasies of him slamming his length into me rushed to the forefront of my mind.

I took it all, wriggling my tongue over the tip and then sucking in and out.

My magic soared through the space around me, tingling in the back of my neck as I pleasured him. His lower body stiffened. He fisted my hair, groaning and panting harder.

"Yaga … fuck, this is incredible."

But then he grabbed my face and pushed me away, leaving me confused.

"It's time to consummate our marriage, my Queen. Get off the pool and go on all fours. I need to claim your sweet cunt now. I waited too long for this." His voice was harsh and low.

I shook my head. Considering his size, once again I wasn't so sure it would work. I rose back on my feet and then walked slowly out, the water was dripping over my naked body when I lowered myself on my fours.

He didn't give me any time to think about this, because he rushed out off the pool quickly and then he he situated himself behind me. Veles started rubbing my ass with his large fingers and teasing my back entrance. I was so wet for him, filled with both anticipation and worry about how he was going to feel inside me.

"Veles," I reiterated. "I'm scared you might hurt me."

"Yaga, your pussy is dripping with your juices. I promise it won't. I'm going to make you remember this forever," he whispered, rubbing my clit. Then, he shoved his hard, long cock into me without warning and I cried out for I thought he was going to tear me apart.

"Fuck, you're so tight, but so very soaked for me," he rasped, brushing my other hole with his free hand. I shivered, feeling myself growing wetter as he began to move.

I whimpered in discomfort, so I asked him to stop. He slowed a bit and continued to rub my back entrance until my whole body tingled with wild energy.

At first, pain and pleasure mingled as he set a slow and steady rhythm. I savoured the feeling of his thumb rubbing that sensitive spot between my ass cheeks.

When I'd adjusted to him, he sped up the pace, reaching under me again to flick my clit with his fingers at the same time.

"Veles, please ... it's too much," I groaned.

"You're mine. Your body and soul belong to me. Do you understand that, Yaga?" he roared, pulling his shaft and then thrusting hard again until I saw stars.

He needed to stop or I was going to pass out.

Then he put his arms around my waist and lifted me up, maintaining his drilling pace. The warmth of his cheek felt soothing against mine.

"I want you to say out loud that you're mine," he growled possessively. My magic bonded with his, as though our cells joined to become one.

I was sure we had company now.

"Yours... only yours," I whispered as a tear rolled over my cheek.

He pinched my nipple and then fucked me faster. Then I screamed his name when another orgasm shattered my walls, hitting me like a firestorm. My breasts bounced as I milked him until at last, his body went rigid and with an unholy growl, he filled my cunt with his seed.

Light shot out of my skin, my arms and legs, until the sensation became unbearable.

What was he doing to me? He was claiming my magic as his while beating my sex with his hand. Everything slowed and this ecstasy I was experiencing now made me so weak. The flame of desire burned, spreading around my heart.

He finally let go of me and I fell on marble floor, lifeless, numb, and fucked.

"Mine, my Yaga," I heard him say before I drifted away to the sounds of his shallow breaths.

CHAPTER II
JADWIGA

I flickered my eyes open, facing the dim light from my bedside table lamp. I had no idea how long I had been asleep, but every part of my body felt sore.

I glanced around the familiar space.

"Impossible," I gasped, certain I was back in my own bedroom in Lviv.

I brushed my hair away from my face. Everything that had happened in the past twenty-four hours couldn't just be a dream. Veles was certainly real.

And when I thought about last night in the washroom, a tremor ran down my spine.

My wand was still in the same spot on the windowsill, so I grabbed it, feeling its energy instantly rush through me. The tips of my fingers burst into flames.

Dream or not, I had let my guard down right before the ceremony in the church, although I never expected to have the god of the underworld, one of the most powerful beings in Slavic history, take Eric's place at the altar. When I tapped into dark magic, I saw a glimpse of my future. Veles needed me to destroy his brother. He had no idea I might possibly be part goddess.

With a heavy sigh, I went to the window, wondering what was going to happen to me next. The Flask of Nightmares was lost forever and with this potion my only chance of becoming a mother was gone, too. Veles had to find another way to help me.

I tried to stand, unsteady on my legs. The memory of what he did to me had me longing for more … so much more. My head still reeled from the incredulity of it all, trying to process this utter yearning that wouldn't leave me be. A yearning for him to possess me, over and over.

Veles was a skilled lover. His sexual torture was at a level I'd never imagined possible. He'd claimed me as his and now, I couldn't stop thinking about his hard cock inside me.

I tried to steady my breathing as my overwhelming magic knocked a few books off my dressing table. I didn't think he was done with me yet, so why on earth did he just return me to my home?

"Get yourself together, Jadwiga," I muttered to myself when I suddenly felt no longer alone.

"Yes, good point. Get dressed because I am supposed to be your guide around Nawia," came a woman's voice.

The door to my room was wide open and she was leaning over the frame, staring at me.

I was wearing my nighty, the one I'd had since my mother passed away several years ago. She, on the other hand, looked perfectly put together and striking.

"How did you get in here?" I asked, charging my hands with magic. She glanced at my sparkling hands and lifted her eyebrow as if to say she wasn't going to harm me.

The woman wore brown leather pants and a black top that revealed her enormous breasts. Her long black hair was smoothed in a ponytail at the back. Stunning was an understatement, and I suddenly felt a tad underdressed.

Recognition struck me then. She was Mokosh, the goddess of fertility. She must have figured out that I'd failed in brewing the Flask of Nightmares and maybe she was here to help me again.

"I have always been Veles' right hand and on Earth, people know me as Lucia," she said lazily, giving me a long, intense look. "I am really sorry about your potion. Veles told me that you were taken by Chernobog."

Her words filled me with sadness but I told myself that all that was in the past and I couldn't change it now. The Flask of Nightmares was lost forever and I still had my gift inside me.

Was she Veles' woman? A mistress? A wave of jealousy wreaked havoc inside my gut. But why did I suddenly care if this goddess, Mokosh, had shared a bed with him or not? It was none of my business. I had my own problems to deal with.

She kept watching me when I went to my wardrobe and picked a dress, as well as my favourite blue cloak. I used my magic to change quickly, wondering how we were going to get to Veles. Perhaps we'd go to an area inhabited by witches who'd found some sort of passage to Nawia—that was the only reasonable explanation.

"Where are you taking me?" I asked.

Her eyes glowed like neon lights.

"Veles is a little preoccupied right now, so he asked me to take care of you," she explained. "Come on, let me show you Nawia, his underworld kingdom."

My jaw dropped and my heart skipped a beat.

"Nawia?" I asked, looking around. "I thought we were in my flat in Ukraine."

She laughed, as though she'd just heard a funny joke.

"It's an illusion—another realm—so we are not in the Ukraine. Apparently, Chernobog angered Veles greatly when he took you away yesterday and thought this way, you'll be safe. He also wanted you to feel comfortable, so he created this for you," she explained, and my jaw dropped.

Just then, the furniture, books, and space I knew vanished, replaced by an endless stretch of land covered with dust and undulating, shadowy hills and soaring mountains. The sky was breathtaking, reminding me of the northern lights filled with rays of purple, blue, and yellow colours. I remembered being here before in a vision.

"This is Nawia, the underworld?" I asked, thinking I wasn't dead unless ... *No*, I would have known if Veles had killed me. He'd vowed to slice my throat first—but if I was here, then anything was possible.

"Yes, it's where all the souls pass once they die," she said. "Veles has never been interested in any mortal women before. You must be very special if he brought you here."

I started chewing on my bottom lip, thinking about the firelight, my special gift, and my inability to have a child. Chernobog had ruined my last chance and I didn't want to lose hope. I knew that the firelight's magic could help me. I had no idea how yet, but it was the most powerful magic of the gods. It could potentially heal me.

I needed to locate it and figure out a way out of this place, ideally alive and well. No one knew how long Veles was planning to keep me here. No other witch had ever met a god or been taken to the underworld. Nawia was the place where witches passed once they died. Nobody could ever enter it just because they needed to.

"Apparently, I'm important to him. He wants to use me to defeat his brother Perun," I muttered.

Mokosh sensed that I was different and I wanted to see if she could figure it out. She seemed to be completely oblivious to our previous conversation back in the library, the space where

I brewed the potion. It appeared she'd lost some of her memories.

"That's very interesting. Well, he has been trying to get rid of Perun for a long time," Lucia said, giving me a dark smile. "There is something about you that seems familiar. We met before but I can't remember. When I travel between realms, my memories sometimes get muddled up. You desire to be a mother. You want this badly, but there is something blocking it."

This was getting uncomfortable.

"Yes, I have been told I can't have children and since you're the Goddess of Fertility ... well, can you help me? Can you heal me?"

She stared at me for a while and I was hoping that this time I could convince her to take away my gift forever. My heart started to jackhammer inside my chest. I needed to remember that she was more powerful than me, that she could help me.

Moments later, she approached me and placed her hand on my stomach. Warmth emanated from her hands.

"Hmmm, everything seems in the right place," she finally said, and I frowned in confusion.

"I have tried many times and I have been told by multiple witches that I am cursed. Apparently, I will never have children," I explained, trying to stay calm.

She still had her hand on my stomach.

"No, you will be blessed with a child soon enough. You don't need me. Everything is in order here," she said with a mysterious smile.

"But I don't under—"

"Just trust me. I can sense these things," she cut me off. This was very strange and I wasn't sure what to think anymore.

"Veles wants me dead. I don't see how this is going to happen if I won't be alive to experience it," I pressed on.

"Sometimes faith works against our wishes. Something you

may want you shall probably never get, but something you need you might already have," she said.

This didn't make any sense at all but soon enough, Lucia moved away from this conversation and started talking about the beginning of times while showing me around these shadowlands.

We walked through dry, empty land that seemed to stretch for miles. I could have never imagined what the world of the dead looked like until today. Many witches had claimed they'd been in Nawia and now that I'd actually been here, I could see their description was fitting enough. The ground was black, the hills covered entirely by charcoal. Lucia explained that some parts were filled with fiery pits, and others with torture chambers where humans were supposed to suffer for eternity.

Lucia was a talker. She revealed she'd been serving Veles for centuries, and before arriving in Nawia, she'd spent a lot of her time in the mortal world, helping women conceive and taking care of abandoned children.

I threw a question or two at her, trying very hard to steer the conversation over to the firelight until we reached a place filled with many rocks and stones. The smell of burning flesh wafted through the air, making my stomach queasy for a moment. As I looked around, I spotted human bones on the ground.

CHAPTER 12
JADWIGA

"Here we are. Now you don't need to ask any more questions about the firelight because we are in the place where the gate normally opens," she said, pointing at the long path ahead.

My heart skipped a beat, then started racing. On each side of the path were countless—hundreds or maybe even thousands of—burning candles, creating this illuminating path of fire. This place reminded me a lot of a cemetery until Lucia stopped at two large metal poles that were sticking out of the ground.

I felt a little dizzy when I recognised the decapitated head of the god Chernobog attached to one of the poles. Veles must have killed him yesterday, but could a god die? Although his skin had a slightly grey colour, Chernobog looked like he would be alive. An icy chill moved down my spine as I stared at his empty eyes and slightly parted mouth.

Veles had made me forget about the orgy and the god that had held me hostage, and that filled me with relief.

On the other pole sat a shiny black skull, darkness and death radiating from it. That twisted, almost scary magic was pulling me towards the object.

I averted my gaze and swallowed hard, wondering what the future held for me. I didn't wish to think about this for now, but one thing I knew: I wanted to live.

"Where are we?" I asked, my voice barely audible. Veles' scent lingered on my skin and for a split second I thought I heard his smoky voice in my head, too. I glanced around, expecting him to step out of the shadows and surprise me. When he didn't, I felt a little disappointed.

My inner voice scolded me, reminding me that Veles was never going to be the prince riding to me on a black horse, but a demon who wanted to use me to get rid of his brother. I didn't think he could truly help me conceive.

"That's where the gate opens," Lucia explained.

This made sense. The heavy magic I'd felt earlier must have come from the firelight, although I still wasn't sure what it was made of. This energy here was pinching my skin and buzzing in the nape of my neck. I kept staring at the skull … the one from my vision.

If I could get my hands on this kind of magic then I would have near-unlimited power—maybe even become immortal and healed.

Lucia chanted some spell in Latin and then the skull started burning with bright fire. The air became dense, heated with her energy and that from another unknown source that I could only sense, not see.

"So, what does the skull do?" I asked, curious.

"The skull holds the firelight in one place and then opens the gate to the other side," she stated.

I nodded, finally making sense of it all. My left palm started to itch and sting with magic.

"Fascinating, so how does the gate open exactly?"

"A specific spell is required, and then your willingness and strength. The firelight connects the gate with the souls on the other side so they can cross over," she went on.

A strong wind started blowing out of nowhere and a flowery scent carried to me. Then, a large, round wooden door appeared between the two poles, which I assumed was the famous gate in the literal sense. Heavy, dark energy surrounded it. I could barely contain my excitement as the door began to open.

Behind it was just blackness.

"The souls should be passing through soon." Lucia giggled, rubbing her hands together as though she couldn't wait for the tortures to begin. I hoped I wouldn't have to witness any of it.

"And who do we have here? Who is this lovely creature?" a new voice chimed in, making me jump.

I glanced to my right to see a man or maybe another god who was literally burning, red flames covering his bare arms and chest. For a moment I thought there was something wrong with my sight, but he was real.

He was also as tall as Veles. It seemed that all the gods were good-looking, but I didn't know why I was even surprised. They were ethereal beings.

"Svarog? What are you doing here? I thought you were in charge of the gate on the other side?" Lucia asked in annoyance.

As soon as she said his name, I recognised him as the god of fire, which made perfect sense.

Svarog fixed his turquoise eyes on me and rubbed his jaw. He studied me from head to toe and I felt myself flushing, the warm sensation travelling to my upper thighs.

"I came to welcome all the women," he replied, his gaze never leaving me.

"I doubt there will be any women today. This is Jadwiga and she's the property of Veles, so stay away from her," Lucia stated, placing her hands on her hips and giving the god a warning look.

Moments later, a few fragile-looking souls started crossing over through the gate, so Lucia needed to direct them to wherever they were supposed to be going next.

And she was right—there weren't any women, only men.

"You're intriguing and very beautiful," Svarog stated, taking a few steps towards me. His flames were fascinating as they didn't seem to hurt him at all. As the master of fire, he was probably immune to his own fiery magic.

"Thank you," I said, tossing my hair to the side and getting closer to him. Since he was in charge of the fire, he would probably know how to create the firelight. As Lucia explained, I needed to have that skull, learn the spell, and then manifest the desire to open the gate. That seemed easy enough—well, at least that's what I wanted to believe. "I heard many incredible things about you. The God of Fire…"

"I thought I was the least famous god amongst mortals?" He laughed, lowering his gaze to my lips, then down to my cleavage.

"Lucia mentioned you are in charge of the gate in the mortal world…" I said casually, tempted to run my hand over his inflamed chest.

"Yes, I create the passage to the other side and I do have the firelight," he explained, looking equally interested in me. "So, tell me, beautiful creature, how did Veles find you?"

I smiled, still mesmerised by the flames. I didn't move when he reached out to run his thumb up my jaw, then down to my lips. His touch was so gentle and a shiver ran down my spine, heating my blood.

And when he put his finger in my mouth, my breathing quickened.

Fuck, the gods must have special powers to make any woman fall at their feet ... all hot and bothered.

All I wanted was to touch his cock and milk it dry…

"I can smell your excitement, mortal woman," he whispered,

and although the fire around his arms touched me, the flames merely teased my skin.

I hesitated, wondering if this was a test, but then this urge made me obey him, so I sucked on his thumb. His skin tasted of fire, something acrid, and smoke.

For a moment, I thought I was back in the washroom, sucking on Veles' cock and running my tongue over his length, then over the tip.

"Good girl, you're such a good witch," he murmured, shutting his eyes.

I felt his other hand moving slowly down to my hips, then he lifted my dress, his fingers roaming under it. His touch felt hot on my skin, the warmth seeping all the way to my chilled bones.

I moaned, still sucking on his finger while he caressed the bare skin on my upper thigh, moving his forefinger inside my damp knickers, over my throbbing flesh. My primal instinct told me that this was a very, very bad idea, but I couldn't stop myself. I wanted to please him. I needed more from him.

"I see you've acquainted yourself well with the God of Fire already," a familiar voice pulled me back from this nightmare.

I almost choked upon seeing an unknown face in front of me while I engaged in a sensual session with the god.

Embarrassed and humiliated, I quickly pulled the finger out of my mouth. The last thing I remembered was standing in front of this beautiful, fiery god, and now he had his hand under my dress, masturbating me.

I yanked his hand away, breathing hard.

"You ... you!" I shouted, pointing at him. "You have charmed me ... what the hell is wrong with you gods?!"

I glanced at Veles, who appeared to be highly amused, then slapped Svarog's face. The god of fire chuckled.

In the distance, Lucia was still guiding souls to their ash chambers. As I later learned, these were places where the souls would confess their greatest sins. Nawia was full of surprises and traps.

Meanwhile, here I was, unable to stop. Svarog must have used compulsion on me. Fuck... Was I so weak then?

"I only wanted to fulfil your desires, witch, and you gladly obeyed," he argued, his searing turquoise eyes trained on me. Then, he pressed some sort of necklace that hung over his chest and the firelight inside the creepy skull suddenly stopped burning.

"I would be careful, brother ... unless you want to end up like Chernobog. He too tried to claim Yaga," Veles warned, pointing at the empty eyes of the God of Faith, whose head was now attached to a metal pole. "So, I wouldn't recommend it."

CHAPTER 13
VELES

It had been a few days since I claimed Yaga's body in the washroom back in Slovenia, in the mortal world. She was mine and now my plan was clear. I had to take her magic because I couldn't have her heart. She was bound to me, but she wasn't falling for me quickly enough. I didn't think I could bring myself to do it, especially now after I tasted her, after we consummated our marriage.

She didn't realise that several days had passed since we got married. To her, this had only felt like a few hours and for now, she didn't need to know the truth. Maybe that was the problem. My powers of illusion didn't work with her yet; if they did, that wasn't the route I wished to take.

I wanted her to love me of her own volition.

However, in reality, I needed to put distance between us because she was becoming a distraction—a novel feeling to me. Unlike other women—be they goddesses or demons—Yaga was making me question everything: my eternity, my purpose, and my sense of life as a god.

I had stayed away from her but that itch to be close to her

was constantly there. Tonight, I was planning to dine with her at a special place. She'd see the real me because we had a connection.

She would love me.

When I entered the place where the gate was located and saw her sucking on my brother's finger, I was furious. I wondered how Svarog had managed to get close to her.

Suddenly, that erotic image of her sucking my cock in that washroom left me with an unholy craving.

Svarog liked playing with both mortal women and his food. We all had different abilities and my brother was a master of fire and compelling others to do his bidding. I had put him in charge of the gate on the other side, and the firelight.

For some reason, the sight of them had me entertaining the idea of Svarog and me with Yaga in the bedroom while she begged me to take care of her. And that made my cock hard.

"Where have you been, Veles?" she asked in anger. She was so beautiful when irritated. Her magic filled with light. "It's all your fault that he used his magic on me. You should have been here to protect me. We are married and you claimed me as yours."

I arched an eyebrow, lobbing my gaze between the both of them. My brother seemed amused, but also curious. He was much more civilised than Chernobog. That was why I allowed him to live.

In the past few days, I wanted to prove to myself that this mortal witch didn't mean anything, that she was simply my weapon in destroying my brother, but now things were more complicated. Her potion was lost and I should have done more to protect it.

"Other things needed my attention, my dear Yaga. I have been trying to find the way to give you what you so desperately desire," I said. The truth was that I felt hopeless because I wasn't sure what I could do. Jadwiga wanted to conceive and I yearned to possess her, body and soul.

I chose to stay away from her because I found myself losing common sense when we were close—whether for minutes or for hours. She was constantly on my mind like no one in the past.

My goal had been clear from the start and now I wondered if I could actually carry it out.

"Use the firelight, Veles. Its magic could make me fertile," she said, glancing back at the black skull.

I frowned, following her gaze, then glanced back at Mokosh. She seemed lost in her thoughts.

"I don't think the magic from the firelight could change you," I stated. "Svarog and I don't know how else it could affect you if we used it to take away your gift."

She bit her bottom lip, her face creased in thought.

"Gift it to me. Make me the mistress of the firelight," she finally said. "Its magic will make me immortal and then the curse that has been cast on my family shall be lifted."

"This makes sense, but you will lose your connection to the mortal realm, Veles," Svarog pointed out.

I was willing to gift her anything she asked for, but firelight was an ancient magic that connected Nawia with the mortal world.

"I will think about this, Yaga. I brought you here because I wanted to show you where I have spent my eternity. I wanted to make you feel welcome," I said, and she laughed.

"That doesn't change anything. You kidnapped me because you figured you could use me in your fight with your brother. Then you used my body in whatever ways you saw fit, and now you're pissed because I have a voice to express how much I'm fed up with the way you've been treating me. Well ... screw you, God of the Underworld. Screw your over-the-top ego. Kill me now because I am never going to submit to you! Never!"

That was a lot of words and just as many unnecessary lies. Yaga didn't realise, but she had already submitted to me—albeit not entirely. This wasn't exactly what I had in mind when I decided to make her mine.

A muscle ticked in my jaw. More blood rushed to my cock and made it stiffen, desperate for me to sink it in her wet hole.

We didn't need to talk because it was easier for me if I didn't know her that well.

"I hate to disappoint you, but I cannot kill you yet because as you said, you need to submit to me entirely and I'm going to do that right now. Brother, are you going to join us?" I asked Svarog, who was busy with the gate and the firelight.

He had been useful in the past and now he needed to be rewarded.

"Join you? No … no … he's not taking part in any of these masochistic things you planned for me. Kill me fucking now, Veles, and get it over with. Do you hear me?!" Yaga yelled.

Then she was in front of me, hitting me with her fists, chanting magic and trying really hard to hurt me.

"Don't waste your energy now, *serce*. You will need it for later." I held her arms as she panted with exertion.

I snapped my fingers, not waiting for my brother's answer. Soon enough, Nawia, the gate, and the endless land vanished.

We were back in the manor, in her bedroom, and it was time to show this girl a good time.

Time for her to submit to me.

Jadwiga

. . .

I was so furious that Veles just left me with Lucia. He never cared about me and now I was in so much trouble because I couldn't control my stupid mouth.

Everything disappeared and I was back in the manor bedroom where I woke up the day after he kidnapped me.

I cursed under my breath, looking around at the dozens of lit candles scattered around the room.

Veles and Svarog were both here and when I glanced at them, sudden heat surged through my veins and made my cheeks flush.

"Undress now," Veles ordered, rolling up his shirt sleeves.

I swallowed hard, trying to think fast. I'd made him angry and that didn't help my situation.

"No, I do not consent to whatever you intend to do," I told him. I had to stand my ground, but anticipation spread stubbornly within me.

I wanted to ignore it, but I couldn't as my fingers tingled with magic. Veles' eyes moved down to my lips, the heat from his gaze making my skin burn with desire.

When he took a few steps towards me, he seemed calm and collected, but my heart was pounding like crazy.

"You see, I don't think this is true, Yaga. My brother and I ... we can sense your desire, your need and want. Your pussy is already dripping wet for both of us," he whispered, leaning close to my ear. He didn't even touch me yet, and he was right. I was so aroused, so turned on, and every nerve in my body reacted to his magic. "Take all your clothes off. We both want to have you naked on the bed. You need to be punished first for your disobedience."

I shook my head, reminding myself that I needed to stand my ground, that despite everything he said, I knew he would never force himself on me. I wanted him back in that washroom. I wanted him inside me like I did then.

At the same time, I hoped he wouldn't use compulsion on

me because I needed to be aware of everything he would do to my body, even if unpleasant.

Sweat formed on my brow. I unbuttoned my dress and let it fall to the floor. I didn't have a bra on, so I stood in front of them in my black lace panties.

Veles' eyes shimmered with raw fire as I glanced up at the two gods who were ready for anything.

The thrill of this game thrummed through my veins and my knees weakened underneath me. I told myself that this wasn't going to be enjoyable, that I didn't want him to possess me again, but these were just lies.

Then, Veles moved closer and cupped my breast. I gasped when his thumb rubbed my hardened nipple before pinching it hard. My stomach tightened with excitement and endless possibilities of what this evening might bring.

"Get on the bed on all fours," he threw another order at me.

I obeyed and didn't even know why I wasn't saying no. My ass in the air, I sensed them both hovering around me, watching and waiting. Shit … this was going to be painful, but at least I was going to experience some kind of sexual pleasure tonight before I died, so that wouldn't be such a bad deal after all.

"She has such a fine ass, brother," Svarog stated when rough fingers caressed my backside.

"She has, but can you smell her desire? She keeps fighting it, but she wants me to bury myself inside her until she forgets her fucking name. She's just so ready to be punished," Veles growled and then ripped my black lace knickers off me.

I yelped in fear and anticipation, aware of the throbbing around my sex.

Then he climbed onto the large bed, right next to me, his warm breath on my skin.

"Tell us, Jadwiga, how many times would you like me to

punish you?" he asked in a whisper while dipping one of his fingers into my wet folds … and oh, fuck, that felt good.

"Four," I croaked as he started moving two fingers inside me. I had no idea why I said that, but the thought of him spanking me was more than alluring. I didn't even realise I was so wet, so primed to receive anything he was giving me.

"You're so soaked, dripping for me, and you smell incredible," he went on, thrusting hard and fast. Then he started licking my clit at the same time. It had to be him.

The pressure in my hips and in the pit of my stomach was suddenly unbearable. I knew I was going to come in seconds, so I pushed my hips towards his hand, panting and forcing myself to stay quiet.

Raw magic swirled in my bloodstream as I gripped the clean sheets, on the verge of exploding.

And then, when I was on the edge, ready to be hit with the biggest orgasm of my lifetime, Veles pulled out and slapped my ass cheeks hard.

The sudden sharp and burning pain made me cry out. My throbbing sex was pulsating and if he would have just touched me there now, I would have come apart in seconds.

"Count, my dear Yaga," he ordered, shifting on the bed somewhere behind me. Svarog must have approached from the other side for I felt him behind me, too, and then his surprisingly cold fingers trailed over my asshole.

"One," I said, my voice filled with frustration and pain.

He slapped me again, this time harder, and I was surprised my knees didn't give out under my weight. The burning pain drove me insane, on top of the fact I was fucking frustrated that he didn't finish me off.

"Two."

"You're such a good and obedient witch," he growled, dipping his fingers into my pulsating sex again.

"Fuck," I moaned, trying not to think about his huge dick ramming into me.

I was ready to come again when Veles withdrew his fingers. Then, Svarog started to rub my back entrance, slowly trying to stick his finger in there until I was slapped the third time.

I screamed in pain as my skin there was on fire, mainly with the effects of them withholding my orgasm.

"Three," I croaked, feeling tears starting to spill down my cheeks, but then Svarog plunged his finger into my bum hole, roughly and without any warning. My head reeled with the contact as he started to pull it in and out, growling loudly. I glanced back, noting Veles had taken off his shirt and was watching me like a hawk. His eyes shone with savage lust.

"No, no, no … please," I begged then as his brother stuck two fingers in my backside. The pressure around my pussy was so potent, it was actually more frustrating than unpleasant.

"Stop denying yourself this pleasure, woman. You want me to fuck you in there. See how wet you are for me," Svarog said, and I felt myself dripping.

I was just about to come from his stimulation of my back entrance. My hips were shaking and my sex demanded attention.

"Just like that … just—"

He stopped then and I growled in irritation, hurling curses at them until Veles delivered his final slap on my ass. My entire backside ached like hell. I thought I could resist this pain, but no … this was too much. *He* was too much. All my senses were on overload.

At that point, I couldn't hold back from crying. I slumped forward, dejected and bruised, breathing in and out and trying not to lose it.

Then I felt something cold, like a cloth, around my backside.

"Now … now, Yaga. You're such a good girl," Veles said, his voice tense and rough. I couldn't fucking take this anymore.

They were both psychos, denying me this pleasure. Death had to be better than this torture. "Stop spilling your precious tears. You need to receive this punishment. And you know that yourself."

"Please, Veles, let me go," I pleaded, thinking I couldn't possibly love this monster. I didn't even know where these strange new emotions came from all of a sudden and why I even thought about it now. This wasn't possible. I fucking hated him. I wanted to kill him for what he had done to me. Him and Svarog.

"But why? The night is still young. We still have so much pleasure to give you," he said, hovering somewhere behind me.

He must have been using magic to soothe the skin around my ass cheeks because the pain was slowly easing, and the burning had stopped. The god of the underworld was healing me, after punishing me.

"Do you want to feel Veles' hard cock inside you now, woman, while I fuck your other hole with the blade handle?" Svarog asked then and I just stared at him, mouth agape. For a split second I thought I must have misheard him. Did he really just say that he was going to fuck me up the ass with the blade handle?

"Fuck," I whispered, wiping the sweat off my brow and realising he wasn't joking.

CHAPTER 14
VELES

I thought this was going to be easy, that I would punish her for her smart mouth, then spank her a few times before my cock entered her slick pussy. And that would be it. But every time she let go of a gasp, moan, or cry, my heart thudded in anticipation.

I spanked her harder than I intended, then I saw tears in her eyes and felt like I needed to burn in my own pit. This had never happened to me before. I had never cared for anyone. I was used to torturing humans in Nawia, so this completely blew my mind.

I had to rectify the situation, so I used my magic to ease her pain, questioning why I'd let my brother join us. All I wanted was to claim her ass for myself.

Yaga became my new addiction, a soul I couldn't get separated from. I couldn't imagine spending another second without her and that was a huge problem. This was going to complicate matters unless I pulled myself together.

And equally, I wanted nothing more than to keep punishing her. She enjoyed it. She demanded the release and I couldn't wait to give it to her.

My brother Svarog stood on the other side of the bed, his erection nearly ripping through his trousers as he ogled my Yaga. He held an iron blade in his hand, the handle made from amber stone, swapping it from one hand to the other.

Then, bright flames appeared on his chest and arms. I took several deep breaths, shutting the doubts in my head as I focused on Yaga's ass and her glistening pussy. Wet for me.

She was so close to experiencing the most intense orgasm ever, yet I couldn't let her come just yet.

Damn, that woman was truly a performer.

I dragged my hand through my thick hair and climbed on the bed once again, ready to finally fuck her until she forgot her name. It was time to claim that pussy, to then give her the satisfaction she desired. I started to unbuckle my trousers while pondering how incredibly tight she must be. A shiver of anticipation wracked me.

Svarog approached as soon as I released my cock. Rock hard, I dipped it slightly in her cunt, teasing her. She whimpered when my brother's flames made the room glow.

Then, Svarog opened a brown flask and started pouring warm oil all over Yaga's backside. Her skin glistened like diamonds.

She sighed, and her whole body shuddered in anticipation and need.

"How much do you want this, Yaga?" I asked her, not recognising my own voice as I gently pushed my cock into her entrance, then tested her back hole with it. She felt glorious.

"Please … just fuck me already," she demanded, her voice hoarse. She must have quickly forgotten about my punishment and I didn't feel guilty anymore.

That's the Yaga I liked. I turned my attention to Svarog who was now massaging his cock with a deft hand.

I plunged my shaft deep into her tight hole and she screamed, belting out a series of incoherent words.

She felt so incredible, tight and wet—her slick cunt took it all as I thrust hard and fast, unable to stop myself.

"Do you like that, Yaga? Do you want Svarog to fill your other hole, too?" I asked, thinking I wasn't going to last long.

I kept sliding my cock in and out until she shouted out for more.

Flames of desire burned through my chest as I grabbed her hips and thrust inside her. She moaned, pleading for more, asking me to go faster until Svarog slipped the blade's amber handle slowly into her well-oiled ass.

This was so fucking arousing. I had never been so hard before in all eternity. My member was like a rock ramming into her cunt.

Svarog growled, fucking her in the ass with his blade handle and pleasuring himself at the same time. Soon… I could sense how close she was—she would reach her climax at any moment.

I, on the other hand, found myself lost in these incredible mortal sensations, experiencing everything she was feeling then.

Then, with all the strength I had in me, I pulled out of her hole, for she knew by now that I owned her pleasure. She'd come when I was ready.

Svarog ejaculated all over his hand and then pulled the blade out of her ass. We were both panting and she crashed on the bed, turning to look at me in confusion and pain. Her chest rose and fell in rapid movements.

Seeing the pain in her eyes shattered my soul and I didn't even know I had one.

"What are you doing, Veles?" she asked, her tone accusatory.

"Beg me to fuck you, my Yaga. Beg for my cock," I told her, and she parted her lips slightly, hesitating.

"Please, Veles, fuck me hard," she finally said, her voice like honey, sweet and seductive.

"Do you love my cock? Did you love that blade ramming into your tight asshole?" I asked through gritted teeth as I was fucking tired of waiting. She was mine, only mine, and now it was time to end this.

"Please ... please, my master," she pleaded, spreading her legs wide for me. Her pussy was gushing, juices spilling everywhere, so I thrust my cock inside her once again.

This was going to be quick. She was taking it so well, moaning so loudly. I pumped my cock into her with everything I had, and she screamed my name, begging me to let her orgasm at last.

So, I did. I released her pleasure, ejaculating my seed deep into her as heat ravaged my cells.

When I finally pulled out, she lay there with a huge smile on her face, trying to catch her breath until Svarog walked up to her.

His cock was still hard, but the needy bastard wasn't going to stick it in her. He was here to witness my possession only and maybe to please her a little, too.

He lifted his hand and stuck his fingers in her mouth.

"Suck your juices, woman, for you belong to the god now," he said, and she obeyed.

Jadwiga

I sucked on Svarog's fingers as though my life depended on it. He must have dipped his hand in wine because I could taste it on my lips.

Both gods were savage, but Veles was all-powerful.

He ordered Svarog to leave and I thought he was going to continue fucking me alone, but he had other plans. I was surprised when he lay in the bed with me and brought me close.

I was too exhausted to move but what an incredible night. Veles had worshipped my body to the point I thought I'd died and gone to Nawia.

"I have enjoyed that closeness, Yaga. I'm glad you finally accepted you're mine," he whispered in my arms, our sticky bodies flush together.

I didn't feel disgusted. I was somehow ecstatic that he was here with me, perhaps wanting more. To get to know me. To keep me.

Something unexpected.

He started whispering things in my ear then, things that couldn't have been real, so I figured I had to be dreaming until darkness obscured my vision. I drifted away into a deep, long, and very pleasant sleep.

I woke up several hours later when it was still light outside, knowing that I was back in the manor, in the same bedroom where he had claimed my body and soul.

My muscles were so sore ... well, my whole body felt like someone had knocked me over several times. Last night had been indescribable.

Someone had dressed me in a soft white tunic. I was still exhausted and when I caressed the skin on my neck, I felt marks there.

Confused and scared, I went to the mirror to see that Veles had marked me everywhere as though he wanted to send a message. Small bites and long scratches from his nails ran over my neck, collarbone, and arms. I didn't remember him doing any of this last night, for I'd been so lost in the moment.

I didn't know why I wasn't upset now. After all, he'd spanked me and made me beg him for release.

Well, I was livid but only for a moment and then I told myself I must have truly lost my mind, because I fancied myself in love with him.

When a knock sounded on my door, I quickly ran my hands through my tangled hair and made myself look decent.

"Come in," I said, getting back on the bed. I knew it was him before he even opened the door.

Veles' tall posture made my knees weak. A heated tangle of desire rushed through my core.

And surprisingly, he gave me a bright smile.

"Hello, Jadwiga, I brought you a late lunch," he informed me and then two dwarves wheeled the small trolley laden with delicious food inside my bedroom. My mouth watered and my stomach growled.

Veles looked so handsome in a crisp white shirt and grey trousers.

Heat rushed to my cheeks, happiness striking me like holiday lights as memories from the night before began spinning in front of my eyes.

This was so wrong, on so many levels. He forced me to marry him, messed with my head and done the most unimaginable things to my body. Then he decapitated one of his brothers before inviting the other to fuck me with a knife handle. And now I started developing feelings for him.

No, this wasn't happening.

"Thanks, so you are trying to be pleasant to me before you ask me to use my gift for you?" I asked, and then instantly regretted it when his smile faded.

Damn, I should bite my tongue. His gaze cut into my skin.

There was no doubt I was attracted to him. I couldn't escape the lust even if I tried.

"I'm not really sure what I mean to do with you, Yaga. Let's eat and talk. Can we do that for now?"

His answer surprised me. He was gentle and in a way, kind like when I met him for the first time at the altar.

"Sure," I replied, because I still wanted to get my hands on that firelight and I could already tell Veles was questioning whether he wanted to let me live or die. The past several hours or days—I wasn't really sure how much time had passed since he forced me to marry him—Veles must have changed.

For a moment, none of us said anything, so I decided to ask a question.

"Are you still in Nawia or you've taken me somewhere else?"

He poured me some tea and then handed me the warm drink. My tunic slipped upwards, revealing my naked thighs, and Veles' gaze wandered down. Tension filled the room as lust oozed off him.

I thought then that the man who sat in front of me could ride me every day and I would never get bored of him.

"I moved us over to the centre of Slovenia," he stated, his voice full of smoke. "I suppose you have never travelled beyond the borders of your country?"

"Yes I have, but it was mostly northern Europe. I was very devoted to my school. I wanted to develop my magic and abilities." Veles didn't need to know how many times I'd risked my life just to learn things that were forbidden, although he knew about my propensity for darkness already. I really wanted to return to the academy. There was still so much I needed to do.

"After centuries in Nawia, aren't you bored of it? Bored of so many souls that are passing through the gate every day?"

For some reason, I'd wanted to ask this question for a very long time. Immortality intrigued me—a god's magic was powerful and so complex. And apparently, I was part of their world although I still wasn't sure how I felt about it.

Maybe he would never admit to feeling lonely or vulnerable at some point in his long life. Veles picked up the meat from his plate and popped it into his mouth. He started chewing, his expression thoughtful.

"No, I don't get bored. There is always something to do in Nawia. Besides, I don't want to be remembered as a second god," he admitted, giving me a long, intense look.

Then, for a moment, we both continued to enjoy the food that had been prepared for us. I didn't think Veles was honest with me—obviously, as god of the underworld, he wasn't happy. But what was missing from his existence?

Was it love? Could he love someone like mortals could?

"And do you think if I help you to destroy Perun, will then everything will change for you?" I pressed, feeling the rising tension in my shoulders.

He now possessed my body and soul, but would he be able to let me go?

"I think you're very valuable just the way you are now. And I don't believe I want to end this."

CHAPTER 15
JADWIGA

I sat there staring at him, trying to digest what he said. Raw fire brewed in my core, slowly spreading around my body.

Then, before I could ask any more questions, he got up and left the room, leaving me sitting there, dumbfounded. I wasn't expecting that. We weren't even done with our conversation yet and he just left. What the hell was wrong with him?

I went to the door and opened it, but the long and dark corridor was empty.

"Veles?" I called out after him, but there was no response. He might be a god, but he acted like a spoiled little child.

He most likely hated that I could see through his soul, see the real Veles and not the God of Nawia.

As my energy heated, a few vases burst to smithereens and all the lights on this floor began to flicker.

I breathed in, telling myself I didn't need to get mad. Veles wasn't going to change. At least not because of me.

I suddenly lost my appetite and decided to explore the manor. I didn't know how long Veles was planning to give me this silent treatment, but he had to come back eventually.

I went to the second floor, admiring the paintings of families that had lived in the manor before he claimed it as his. The heat from my magic was making me a little uneasy. Another voice inside me whispered that soon enough, I would have to make a huge decision that could affect the future of the entire Kingdom of Opana. My throat clogged with emotion.

As I stood staring at the paintings, a sudden awareness crept over my spine. I was no longer alone and someone was watching me from the shadows. I glanced to my right as the warmth shifted, zooming over the surface of my skin. My pulse quickened.

"You have been lost in your thoughts for a little while, woman," the deep familiar voice stated.

I relaxed instantly as I recognised Svarog.

"How long have you been watching me? It's creepy," I chided, walking up to him. Tiny flames burst forth from his shoulders, spreading down to his arms. That was probably a reason why he never wore a shirt—the fire would certainly destroy it.

Damn, Svarog was so good-looking even now in the darkness, but that didn't change the fact that I was most attracted to Veles.

"A little while," he answered. "I like watching humans, especially when I am in the mortal world. They are always so intriguing."

I noticed his necklace, a rectangular vessel shape with an upside-down triangle beneath it. I remembered how he'd touched this necklace before the firelight started burning back in Nawia.

This was probably my chance to find out as much as I could about the firelight magic.

"What do I need to do to get access to the firelight? I would like to be in charge of the gate in the mortal world," I asked, getting straight to the point. I didn't think I needed to do anything to have Svarog on my side. I got that vibe from him that had me suspect he'd help me.

I knew then if I was going to somehow survive this, I couldn't get back to Ukraine empty-handed, especially now after my potion was ruined.

I wasn't planning to waste my life and become his sacrifice without ever having experienced motherhood.

Svarog cocked his head to the side and gave me a devious smile as though he understood what I was planning. Whatever arrangement he had with Veles over the gate didn't really matter. Veles could still get the souls even if Svarog gave me access to it.

"In order to open the gate, you need the skull and this necklace. In addition, I would have to show you how this spell works. It's pretty complex magic," he explained, sounding amused.

"I am aware of that and also of the fact you're the one that could hand me these things in exchange for something else," I said, running my hand seductively over his chest. His fire dimmed and his skin felt so incredibly warm. Lust scorched through me when I thought about last night. He and Veles both made me lose my mind.

"Are you aware that if I do decide to help you, then Veles won't be able to cross over to the mortal world anymore? He will remain in Nawia forever. Once you cross the gate in the mortal world and I transfer its magic to you, he will automatically return to the underworld," Svarog explained, his fiery eyes boring into mine. The fire around his pupils gleamed brightly.

A cold shiver crawled over my spine as I processed what he had just told me. If I was going to steal the firelight from Veles, then he would be stranded in Nawia forever.

I wouldn't care too much; at least then I would get rid of him for good, but the voice inside me questioned if I could really do this? After all, I did have certain feelings for him. Didn't I?

I wasn't entirely sure how I felt about him now.

"No, I wasn't aware of it," I said, then bit my lower lip. With firelight, I could become the greatest witch in Opana and that was very tempting. This way, I could also achieve my greatest goal of becoming a mother.

My father would be so proud of me if he learned I'd tricked the god of the underworld and trapped him in Nawia, just so I could become the gatekeeper and a guide for all mortal souls.

"I want to be in charge of Opana when the time is right. This is my price for the firelight," Svarog said without a hint of hesitation in his voice.

I looked around to make sure nobody was listening. We were alone. Veles was somewhere in the manor, intentionally avoiding me. He had been doing this for a while, only giving me snippets of information, thinking it would appease me.

"You do understand that Opana is governed by the Council. I don't have anything to do with it," I told him, a little baffled that he was interested in governing the kingdom.

I didn't have any vested interest in politics and it was mostly male witches who could become members of the Council. I thought this was the most absurd rule of them all.

"Maybe not for now, but once you're in charge of the gate in the mortal world ... well, that changes everything. This is the price. Give me your promise and I'll hand you the firelight," he said, then took something out of his pocket.

I felt like my legs were going to give out under my weight when I saw the blade with the familiar amber handle—the same one he'd stuck in my ass and then fucked me with while Veles thrust his cock in my pussy.

Heat rushed through my body, so potent and raw I felt like I might just climax in that moment alone.

Svarog ran his hand over the blade, staring at me with pure lust in his eyes.

"Yes, you have my word, Svarog," I said, smiling and ignoring the savage desire I felt for his brother, Veles. He was the one who continued to mess with my body and soul. "But I doubt very much that means anything. He's going to kill me anyway. He's probably already preparing."

"Yes… but let me explain how the spell works. There is a lot that I have to teach you about this magic," he said, and then started whispering all those secret details in my ear.

Veles

I sensed disturbances all around me, so I knew it was finally time. All the creatures in the forest were whispering that other gods had found out about my involvement with Yaga. I couldn't drag this any longer. She had to die. This needed to be the end and there was nothing I could have done to change the course of things.

I rubbed my palms together, knowing that she belonged to me now, that I was in possession of her body and soul.

She'd forced me to walk away from her earlier because when I sat in front of her in that bedroom, I realised I had done this all wrong.

I should have spent more time trying to get to know her first instead of just showing up in the mortal world, then pretty much kidnapping her.

As the storms began to gather in the sky, my chest felt like it cracked open.

"Bring her outside. It's time," I ordered Svarog when he appeared at the door several moments later.

"Are you sure you're ready for this?" he asked, seeming to sense my hesitation.

"Yes, I want her outside now. The other gods should be here soon," I said, after which he left me alone.

I went to the table and drank some ambrosia. I couldn't delay this or change my mind now. I had waited for this moment for centuries.

Perun was finally going to pay for constantly antagonizing me, so I headed outside and, in the distance, I spotted the large pole with the black skull on top of it.

Svarog most probably planned to return to Nawia as soon as I accomplished what was necessary here in the mortal world.

The air was charged with electricity and the dark clouds settled like a heavy weight on my shoulder. I felt the same ache I'd experienced when Chernobog had tried to force himself on my Yaga.

A few minutes later, I inhaled sharply as that discomfort was quickly replaced by a burning sensation when I sensed Jadwiga approaching.

She was walking behind Svarog and in that moment, the muscle inside my chest that humans called the "heart" began to pound faster. She was so beautiful, but she had to die. She had enormous power and only her magic could destroy my brother. My plan was foolproof.

She stopped right next to me, her eyes wary as she focused them on the skull.

"Just get on with this, Veles. I'm tired of waiting," she stated, and I understood. I could have made this easier for both of us.

Beads of sweat ran down my back when the thunderstorm pounded through the sky and the wind blew, ruffling her hair and bringing unexpected cold air. My cock was stiff again. I'd claimed her, but I wanted to do it again, over and over.

I didn't want to kill her.

In the distance, several creatures appeared among the foliage and trees. Vilas, Likho, wolfmen, vampires and other demons had arrived to witness how I'd take power over all the gods and of course, my brother Perun. Time was ticking, moving too slowly as the wind turned into a cyclone. Soon enough, the storm would rip through the manor, tearing tree roots from the ground and destroying mortal villages.

I had the power to stop all this and bring Yaga back to Ukraine.

My skin prickled with her magic. I walked around her and wrapped my arm around her neck, inhaling her incredible scent that sent my heart thumping.

Fuck, her skin smelled like rain, freshly-cut grass, and wildfire. I could hear her heart beating in her chest.

"I'm the master of this mortal realm!" I roared after a moment, and she shuddered in my arms. "I've claimed the witch from the prophecy. Now it's my turn to rule."

I took out the blade Lucia had made for me in the pits of Nawia and pressed it over Yaga's delicate neck. She yelped, releasing that sweet moan through her lips that made me want to rip her clothes off and take her again before I slit her throat. I wanted to bury myself inside her sweet, tight pussy.

Minutes passed and it started raining heavily, even more than during that night when I fucked her in the bathroom.

I brushed my cheek over hers, taking in her scent and enjoying this moment until I had to end her.

She calmed down a little, waiting and her gaze fixed ahead. She'd probably accepted her faith.

We were all soaked minutes later. The wind blew and I was still hesitating. I was waiting for the sign, but there was none. My conscience urged me to proceed—the other gods weren't coming.

I needed that fucking sign though. I wanted to be certain I was doing the right thing. Fury wiped through me like a windstorm, but I pushed it back with a few deep breaths.

Several long moments passed and still nothing happened. The storm was slowly passing, which didn't make sense. Someone must have arrived. Maybe the other gods had realised what I'd been planning all along. Lucia revealed that she was important, but Mokosh was my partner. She didn't need Jadwiga. Apparently, Yaga was a half goddess and that explained why there was such a pull between us. She didn't even realise I'd discovered her secret. She was able to create life and destroy me—the immortal. She had an ember of life within her. I was torn between what I needed and what I desired.

Yaga was shaking and my irritation grew in leaps and bounds. Why the fuck couldn't I fucking go through with it?

I felt like I was being mocked by everyone around us, by nature itself.

More time passed as I forced myself to make that move, to pierce her skin with the blade. To take her life.

The storm passed at last. The tornado must have moved farther up north to other parts of this mortal country.

"Fuck," I snapped, letting the blade fall down on the grass.

I couldn't fucking do it.

I didn't want to kill her, slit her throat, or even snap that delicate neck. I just couldn't bring myself to be separated from her.

I tangled my hand in my hair, stepping away from her. The pain inside my chest spread all through me.

Was this what all mortals felt?

When the soul was ripped from the body?

I didn't know because I had never truly cared about anyone before.

"What happened? Why didn't you do it?"

I heard her voice, but couldn't bring myself to look at her. She must have turned around to face me now.

"I don't fucking want to end your life, my sweet Yaga, and I don't want to use you to end my brother. No one cares that you can wipe all the gods from this earth. No one cares how powerful you truly are!" I shouted, finally managing to meet her gaze. Even wet as she was, she glowed.

Her expression filled with confusion.

"So you're not going to kill me?" she asked carefully, her voice sweet as honey.

I had hurt her, fucked her and punished her. That was wrong … all so wrong.

"No, I can't because I fucking fell in love with you, Jadwiga, and I didn't think I was capable of loving you or anyone. I didn't think love was real until now … until today," I said, compelled to tell her exactly how I felt.

I'd fought with these new emotions since that night bathroom, trying to push them away. I avoided her and only talked to her when I thought it necessary.

There was no point in denying it anymore. I was in love with her. As a god, I wasn't supposed to experience this, but I didn't want to lose her. My heart kept beating inside my chest and when I finally confessed how I felt, she gasped.

Her pupils dilated and her mouth parted. She looked like she wanted to say something, but then just stared at me, her breathing heavy, whizzing.

A long moment passed. I couldn't stand this silence. My mind started racing because I wasn't sure if she would ever forgive me for kidnapping her, for claiming her body and soul as mine.

Then, her face went a little pale and she turned to look at Svarog. My brother was surprised, too.

"I think I'm in love with you too, Veles."

CHAPTER 16
JADWIGA

I felt like the world underneath my feet opened up and the pits of Nawia swallowed me in.

Did the god of the underworld really just confess his undying love for me?

It seemed so hard to believe, yet this wasn't a dream. He really was going to let me live and breathe.

He knew. Veles knew about my vision, about my special gift. I couldn't just imagine this. He also knew about the ember of life and yet, he let me live.

And then I told him I thought I was in love with him, too.

He'd gone so far as to admit he shouldn't have hurt me. He confessed he was in the wrong.

Magic danced inside me and rolled off me in waves.

Excitement filled my whole being.

I never believed I could fall in love with a man, a mortal, or even a witchlord because my father had always told me love could ruin me. His words about love cut deeply into my psyche. He believed it would only bring destruction, sorrow, and death.

He could never understand why I wanted to bring a child

into this world. He kept saying that I had time, that I needed to focus on my magic, that I was destined for greatness.

Children could wait.

I didn't know why he was so against creating a family. I had a feeling that had something to do with my mother. She'd died so young and Dad, well, he never talked about her.

Now I knew my father was wrong. He resented me because he'd lost the love of his life, so that fuelled his treatment of me.

And when the distance between Veles and me vanished and he took me in his arms, everything was forgotten. Then, he just kissed me. There was nothing soft and gentle about that kiss. He devoured me, caressing my tongue with his until a slow moan escaped me.

The heat from his body ignited my blood with his waves of magic. He pressed harder, claiming my lips and leaving me breathless. It was as though he couldn't get enough of me. Or maybe he thought I would pull away and simply end this.

I couldn't because I knew what I wanted now. His hand moved down over my hips, then squeezed my ass cheek.

He paused the kiss and smiled at me, caressing my face.

"You're so beautiful, Jadwiga," he said. "Will you do me the honour of staying here with me?"

"Do you mean here in the manor?" I asked, thinking about my life back in Ukraine, about my family and school.

This whole thing was happening all so fast. I didn't think I could give everything up just for love… Was I capable of something like that?

"Yes, I want to build a new life with you here in Slovenia. Is that too much to ask of you?"

I had to think about this. Surely, I wanted nothing more than stay here, with Veles, but on the other hand, I needed some kind of closure in the place I'd always called home.

"No, it's not. I wish for the same, but I need to get back to the Ukraine first. I have certain mortal things I need to take care of before I start over somewhere else," I explained, breathing in and out, pushing these dark thoughts about the firelight away. I didn't need that power anymore. I had Veles' love and that was suddenly enough.

I hoped Svarog would understand. After all, the god of the underworld had chosen me as his consort.

"Of course, that can be arranged," he replied, kissing first my hands, then my knuckles.

"Well, if I may say something," Svarog said, reminding me he was still here with us, listening to our exchange. "That's unexpected, but I am pleased that this ends well. I have a little surprise for you."

Moments later, I sensed something coming out of the woods. The ground started to shake as I glanced at the forest, wondering if that was Svarog's surprise.

A rumbling sound ensued, as if someone or something large was tearing through the trees, towards us. For a second, I thought I would see a dragon or one of the other large beasts that hide in these woods, but then, shock riddled me.

A hut stomped out from the edge of the forest, appearing to be walking on legs. And they weren't just any legs, but chicken legs.

Veles' pupils dilated and his lips parted in a soft smile when he recognised the hut.

"What is that?" I asked as the cottage moved at a phenomenal speed, then just stopped, lying down on its legs as though it truly belonged in that spot. As though it had always been there.

The house was made of wood with a thatched straw roof and a small chimney. I had never seen anything like it. The hut grounded itself, releasing smog out of the chimney as though it was truly alive. Its magic was strong, pounding and crackling all around us.

"That's the house on chicken legs," Svarog stated. "It's my gift to you, Jadwiga. I thought you might like it. If we go inside, it will take us to Nawia."

I tried to digest everything he just said, but was having trouble understanding why he thought I'd like this. Then, the door of the house swung open and Svarog started to head inside.

Veles gave me a nod and strolled after his brother.

Did I want to enter this magical abode with the brothers? I decided to give it a go.

As soon as I stepped in, the door shut and the whole house lifted itself up. The floor rumbled, the entire structure wobbled. I screamed. Laughter echoed as it first moved, then stilled again.

That had to be the most bizarre experience of my life.

The cottage had a low ceiling and consisted of two rooms. The dark, cramped space smelled of burnt wood, mould, and herbs. We stood in an open-plan room with a huge fireplace and an old mortar hanging above the crackling fire. To the side was an old wooden table with a few chairs. Somehow, I felt good being in this space. It calmed me and made me feel like I was home.

I didn't really understand that feeling as the cottage was dark with tiny windows, and there were several bloodstains on the oak floor.

Veles moved his palm gently over the length of my back and my breath hitched.

Svarog fixed his gaze on me at the same time, holding the pole with the shiny black skull that burned with red flames in his hand.

"Have you created this place, Svarog? Is that how you've been moving around the mortal world? How have you been collecting souls?" I asked.

It seemed as though the house breathed oxygen as the floor moved in sync with the rhythm of my heart.

"Yes, the cottage can charge through the mortal world, taking me to any place I want. However, now it's time for me to leave you both. I must open the gate. The souls in the mortal world are waiting for me, so I must return there now," he said, his eyes sparkling with bright flames.

"I thought we were in Slovenia," I pointed out.

"No, the house must have taken us back to Nawia. I believe Svarog wanted you to experience how he normally travels," Veles explained.

"Right," I muttered.

Soon, the magic began to lift and spread through the whole cottage. Svarog chanted the spells that allowed him to open the gate—the one he'd taught me about earlier on.

The same large wooden door I'd seen when Lucia had shown me around appeared. The impact of the magic blew everything around—books, flasks, herbs and everything else tumbled on the floor as the whole house shook, rumbled, and the crackling fire made a sneezing sound. Veles held me, chuckling when I almost fell on my ass.

I glanced through the tiny window, seeing that indeed we were back in Nawia, the grey and rocky land facing us ahead. The black skull burned with fire and then I felt a weight on my chest.

I darted my gaze down at my cleavage, seeing the necklace with a rectangular vessel shape and an upside-down triangle beneath it that Svarog had worn around his neck. I shot him a surprised look and for an instant, I thought he was smiling.

My throat went dry. The necklace was the only thing I was missing that would allow me to open the gate.

Back at that time in the corridor, he'd agreed to give it to me, but now I didn't need it. I swivelled momentarily to see Veles turn his attention to the gate, his strong hands resting on my arms now. From behind me, he couldn't have noticed I had the necklace.

Suddenly, an icy cold shiver crawled over my spine when Svarog opened the door to the gate. The powerful energy of this passage could not be ignored. I breathed in, held on, and then exhaled.

He was just about to walk through it but then paused to regard me.

"I think this is goodbye. You both have your happy ever after—now it's my turn to rule," he said.

After winking at me, he walked through the darkness, entering the mortal world on the other side.

The gate was open and the God of Fire was gone. Hesitating, I forced myself to take a few steps towards it. Veles let go of me and I felt him shifting slightly, but he didn't follow me.

I wanted to admire the gate for a little while longer, and then I understood my purpose. The magic from the gate was so powerful, it could allow me to become a mother. It could truly change my life and give me the fulfilment I had been yearning for all these years. I expected to see a few souls walking through it until Svarog's words rang in my mind over and over again like an echo.

It's my turn to rule.
It's my turn to rule.
It's my turn to rule.

I didn't understand what that meant until I felt the heavy weight of the shiny skull in my hands. My pulse then quickened as I realised what these words meant.

Svarog had kept his word. He had gifted me the necklace, the skull, and taught me the spell that would allow me to open the gate. He'd give me the firelight, transferred all its powerful magic to me.

"What is on your mind, dear Yaga?" Veles asked, startling me a little.

His tone was surprisingly calm whereas I … well, I suddenly felt empty and numb inside. Yes, I was in love with him, but only then did it hit me. This wasn't enough because I wanted to have a child, maybe even *his* child, but I was certain now the gods couldn't reproduce. Besides, Veles was in love with me already. He wouldn't want to share me with anyone else, and a child could complicate things.

I was in charge of the firelight and I was invincible. This knowledge filled me with life.

Then I saw myself in front of a crowd of witches, all cheering, *"Baba Yaga!"* A witchlord stood next to me. I saw the resemblance—he was my blood. My son, the child I always wanted!

The house on chicken legs took me back to Nawia, and the gate was still open, which meant I could go anywhere. I could go home if I chose to. Veles had no idea what was going on and I didn't think I could just give all that power up for … what … love? Something I couldn't even describe yet?

I wasn't that foolish.

"I'm sorry, Veles. I'm truly, truly sorry, but I won't make you happy. I finally have everything I ever wanted and more. I hope you will forgive me!" I shouted, turning so he could see my face.

He looked confused at first, lost, and then his eyes finally spotted the skull that was burning with bright red flames. The firelight singed my hands, but I didn't care because a split second later, I was walking backwards, crossing the gate and leaving Veles forever. I beat him at his own fucking game. He moved towards me, reaching out for me with a horrified expression on his face.

"Noooooo!"

He could no longer touch me because I had already crossed

over and he couldn't go back to the mortal world for Svarog had transferred the fire magic to me.

I made a choice. I chose darkness and power over love.

And I believed it to be the best decision I ever made.

The End

UNEXPECTED ENGAGEMENT

BABA YAGA'S INSPIRED ROMANCE AND MYSTERY ROLEPLAYING: ONE SHOT ADVENTURE FOR FIFTH EDITION (DND/RPG)

RPG WRITER: ANTONY M COPELAND

UNEXPECTED ENGAGEMENT

Baba Yaga's inspired Romance and Mystery Roleplaying One Shot Adventure for FifthEdition (DnD/RPG)

JOANNA MAZURKIEWICZ

Kingdom of Solace

The Prussian Empire

Vienna

Lubijana
Novo Mesto

Kingdom of Opana

Tuzla

Sarajevo

The Caspian Federation

Kiev

Kingdom of Wallachia

MAGICAL BANQUET INVITATION

Beatrice

and

Dominic

MAY, 25TH, 1968 AT 2 PM

AT ESSU MANOR HOUSE PART OF SLOVENIA PARISH IN KINGDOM OF OPANA

Suprise Party to follow

Thisadventure is intended for a party of 5 level 6 characters and will take about 3-4 hours. They have been invited to a party at the palatial mansion of Duke Dominik Reylander of Vienna.

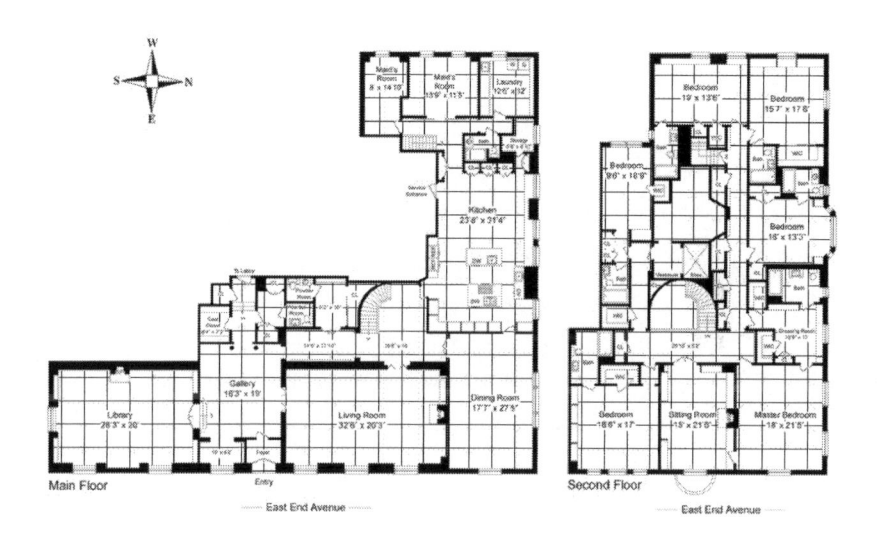

Read this section aloud:

The adventurers are welcomed into the mansion's living room by the house staff and find Duke Reylander standing in front of the mantel.

"Thank you all for coming this evening. I suppose you're all wondering what we're celebrating today," he begins.

"Wine! What else is there to celebrate?" suggests a white-haired old gent among the guests.

"Right you are, Philipp," continues the Duke, "and there will be plenty of wine to be had. I have a vintage I'm sure you'll appreciate."

The guests chuckle politely.

"The real reason you're all here, my closest friends, companions, and associates, is because I have an announcement to make, and not even my dear Beatrice is aware of it." Duke Reylander pauses.

"Beatrice, please stand." The young woman, who has been sitting to the Duke's left, stands up. She looks shy and puzzled.

"What is it, Dominik?" she asks.

The Duke takes her hands in his and kneels down before her. Some of the guests gasp softly.

"Beatrice. Ever since you came into my life, not a day has gone by that hasn't been brightened by your presence. The light of your smile fills my heart with joy, and I find I cannot bear the thought of being without you. Would you please consent to be my bride?"

She looks him in the eyes. The expression on her face is difficult to read. It would seem that she's moved by his words, though someone more cynical might regard it as an expression of pity. A servant comes forward holding a slim black box and opens it to reveal a necklace encrusted with diamonds and sapphires and bearing an interesting design on its pendant. Beatrice casts her gaze briefly on the box, then returns her attention to the Duke.

"Yes," she says at last, smiling affectionately. "Yes, of course I will, Dominik."

The guests clap politely as Duke Reylander puts the necklace on his fiancée. She turns back to him and whispers something in his ear.

"Beatrice would like to change her outfit to better match her new necklace. We can await her in the dining room."

Beatrice practically dances out of the room and heads up the stairs as the rest of the guests are led to the dining room.

As your party and the guests are guided to their seats, the sounds of breaking glass, a scream, and a thud are heard from upstairs.

The servants and several of the guests rush to the source of the noise.

What do you do?

. . .

UNEXPECTED ENGAGEMENT

If the adventurers choose to follow the crowd, they will find themselves in Beatrice's room. The dressing table chair and mannequin displaying her evening gown have been knocked over. The jewelled necklace sits on a jewellery stand on the dressing table. The window next to the bed is broken and the night air blows into the room, carrying the sound of cackling laughter.

"Where is she?" the Duke will ask, looking distressed.

The servants will herd everyone out of the room, asking the guests to wait in the banqueting hall while they clear things up. The banqueting hall will have an elaborate feast laid out, a string quartet and a variety of well-to-do guests who, when asked, will state they know nothing of the bride's disappearance, though some may gossip about her uncertain lineage. A DC 10 Persuasion roll is all that will be required to loosen their lips.

The footmen will politely attempt to keep all the guests—including the adventurers—within the banqueting hall. If they manage to leave, they may explore the rest of the house. The party may attempt to make a Persuasion check or Intimidation check to convince the servants to let them help (DC 13), or try a Stealth check to leave through a window or through the kitchens. Going through the kitchens will be much harder since the area will be staffed. Once outside the building, they may re-enter through the lobby entrance.

The Gallery will be found to contain several imposing portraits of the Duke's ancestors. Many of the guests bear at least a slight resemblance to these gentlemen.

If they return to Beatrice's bedroom, they shall find a chambermaid by the dressing table. She will claim to be clearing up the broken glass, though she is nowhere near the window. She will attempt to excuse herself and leave the room. A perception check or Passive Perception above 11 will reveal that the necklace is missing. A DC 12 insight check may lead them to conclude that the maid took it. They may attempt to stop and interrogate the maid, or they can try to pick her pockets with a Sleight of Hand check. A roll of 12 or higher will recover the necklace.

Investigating the window would reveal a strange odour and a strip of dirty black cloth hanging from a broken, jagged pane of glass. The window looks like it was broken from the outside, but there's little to indicate that the kidnappers scaled the wall. There are no pitons or a climbing rope. There was no ransom note left behind.

The master bedroom will reveal the Duke being consoled by a guest. If questioned, he will know nothing about the abduction. If intimidated, persuaded, or charmed (DC12), he may tell the party that she was not from one of the more well-known contemporary noble houses, but that her family has strong roots in the nation's culture and history. If the party leaves and returns later, they may find the bridesmaid riding the Duke. If confronted, the Duke will seem besotted with the girl. If any of them cast Trueseeing, or have any other means of acquiring Truesight, they will see that the girl is, in fact, a Succubus. The fiend will disappear into the ethereal plane if she knows she's been discovered, leaving the Duke confused and still Charmed by the Succubus, unless the party can snap him out of it. They may do this by casting a Greater Restoration spell or causing him pain, which will allow him to attempt a DC 15 Wisdom saving throw against the charm effect.

After discovering the Succubus, if any of the party goes off on their own, the Succubus will reappear and attempt to charm the lone adventurer. If she succeeds, she will get them somewhere private, such as one of the many bathrooms and closets, and will then attempt to use her "kiss" on them. The DM will try to give the other players plenty of time to potentially catch her in the act.

The party might also be accosted by one of the guests,

Annika Reylander, an older cousin of the Duke. She will tell them not to bother chasing after Beatrice: "Dom can do much better. She's not even real aristocracy! Let her be gone. He'll get over it and we'll find him a better match. Perhaps someone much closer than he realises." The party members would only need to succeed on a DC10 Insight check to realise that she wants to marry the Duke herself.

The library has a selection of books that don't seem to fit among the law tomes and the ones about the history of Opana, including: "The Tales of Baba Yaga", "Everyday Herbalism", "Incantations for Self-improvement", "The Veles Amulet" and "The History of Witchcraft and Witch-hunting". There may even be a Tarroka deck. If anyone in the party should ask a servant or return to the dining room to ask a guest, they will learn that these books and the deck of cards belong to Beatrice.

In the wine cellar (accessible by taking the stairs down from the rear of the kitchen, near the Maids' Rooms and Laundry) they find Philipp helping himself to the best wines. He will happily and drunkenly inform the party that Beatrice comes from a long line of witches that can trace their heritage back to Baba Yaga, and will moan that no one believes in witches anymore. "I don't mean those modern wannabe witches with their incense and music, either. I'm talking the real deal!" An investigation of the far wall will reveal a secret door to a hidden room containing an altar, pestle and mortar, potions, various herbs, a Book of Shadows, and various other trinkets and paraphernalia associated with Witchcraft. If the party asks Philipp about it, he'd say, "I thought that was all just talk among the family. How did she get it all in here? You'd better show Dom. I mean the Duke!"

If they wish to return to the Duke and haven't discovered the Succubus yet, then he will still be in his bedroom with her, and they might interrupt her as she intimately drains the life from him. If they have already saved him from her, then he would be in the dining room with the guests, preferring not to be alone. If the party asks him about the secret room in public, he will deny any knowledge of it and come with you to see it, asking that the other guests remain in the dining room and continue to enjoy the feast. Once he is away from the other guests, he will actually tell the adventurers that he has something to show them, and requests they follow him to his private sitting room on the second floor.

If they found him in the bedroom, he will similarly ask that they come to his sitting room. Once there, he will explain that those items are trophies that he and his family have collected over generations of witch-hunting. Most of the family are kept in the dark about it and are encouraged to think of the old tales of the Reylander Witch-Hunters as nonsense, but it is up to the male heir to continue the tradition. "Beatrice and I actually met on one of my hunts. I had tracked down a foul hag in her lair. The creature had several children in cages. Beatrice was older than the others. An adolescent at the time. She was being forced to fatten the children up, clean out their cages, and when the hag demanded, she'd take a child from its cage and bring it to the cooking pot. Grateful for rescuing her from the hag's tyranny, Beatrice came back to the house with me. I swore to protect her and keep her safe, but she insisted on coming along with me on witch hunts. With her aid, I discovered several more lairs, though we rarely caught any more hags—only lesser witches. Over time, we became quite close."

At this point, the adventurers may attempt to piece everything together. They may make an Insight check DC20, but they get a +5 if they've found Beatrice's books in the library and another +5 if they've talked to Duke Reylander about the secret room. If they succeed then they realise that Beatrice has been playing Dominik all along and that she wanted the necklace. If they want to track down the chambermaid they found in Beatrice's room, they will find out from the other servants that she left in a hurry, through the gardens. They may be able to persuade the Duke to help them bring Beatrice to justice—though he may be too heartbroken to act (roll a Wisdom save for him if you wish).

If they go out into the garden, they may find the gardener (DC15 Perception check as he will likely be among the hedges). If questioned, he will tell the adventurers that he saw three women fly off on broomsticks after the crash of breaking glass, and will give them a direction without much provocation. Alternatively, they can track the runaway maid into the woods.

The stables have horses they may use to reach the hags more quickly. They also find the stable lad getting it on with a maid. They will be embarrassed at being caught, but neither of them is s fiend at this time. If the party wishes to involve themselves in some harmless fun, they'll be able to join in on a DC15 Persuasion check. If they do this, however, they may arrive at the woods too late to stop the ritual (DM's discretion).

In the woods, they may find a pack of 8 Dire Wolves trying to herd them away from the hags. If the adventurers successfully defeat or chase off the wolves, they will be able to hear the chanting and see the fires through the trees. They will find the three hags naked, dancing in a circle, Beatrice bound and naked in the centre. All of them are green-skinned, twisted, bent and ugly, though one will be noticeably older than the other two. They will be chanting and casting various spells over the young woman, burning herbs and spreading lotions on her naked body as she screams. Not the high-pitched scream of the damsel in distress, but a low, guttural cry of pain.

If they step in and try to stop the ritual, they may try to persuade the green hags to let Beatrice go, or choose to fight them. If they roll an 18 or higher for Persuasion, the hags will tell the party that the ritual cannot be stopped, that this is her destiny. Her time has come. The hags will then try to subdue the adventurers.

Have only one of the hags engage in the melee if you can help it. Have this one be the Crone, and if she takes fatal damage, tell the players the following:

The hag, the most wrinkled of the three, reeling from the pain you inflicted on her, staggers over to where Beatrice lies pegged out on the ground. She drops to her knees next to the woman and picks up a knife from the ground.

If the players interrupt at this point because they assume the hag is about to stab Beatrice, that's okay. If they attack the Crone or not, the following will still happen:

The hag's blood spills from her body, splashing across the naked and helpless Beatrice. The old Crone slumps to the ground dead, and Beatrice begins to convulse and twitch. Her skin begins to turn green, her arms elongate, her fingernails become claws, her body twists, her spine becomes bent and crooked, her chin and nose grow sharp, and her mouth widens into a grim smile.

The other two hags will then use their actions to release their new sister. They may attack the adventurers, but before the party is killed, the three of them will try to escape together, turning invisible if necessary and using their Brooms of Flying if they can. However, if the adventurers succeed in preventing the green hags' ritual, then Beatrice will thank them for saving her. If intimidated or persuaded (DC15), she may tell the party that she is hexblood, from a long line of hags and sorcerers, and admit that she had been trying to regain The Veles Amulet. The Crone was reaching the end of her days and it was her time to become the new Maiden, but now the coven is broken; she is truly free to be herself and asks you to escort her back to the Duke.

If the adventurers allow the ritual to continue or are restrained and forced to watch, the eldest green hag will plunge

UNEXPECTED ENGAGEMENT

a dagger into her chest at the ritual climax and spill her blood onto Beatrice's body, then fall down dead. The young woman's skin would then turn green, her features would become ugly, and her sister hags would release her and help her to her feet. As stated earlier, they may then close in on the adventurers, but will try to escape before they wipe out the party or take too much damage themselves. Make it a close call if you can!

If the Adventurers survive the adventure and Beatrice remains unchanged, they may return her to Duke Reylander if they wish, and he will offer them a reward of 1000gp for her safe return, though he may not like it if she returns still naked. There might also be an inquiry into the missing necklace unless it was already returned to him. The conversation between the Duke and his fiancée may vary depending on whether you told him what she was. She is more likely to win him over if the party helps to persuade him. Any attempts to use magic to sway him will result in him yelling, "You have been found guilty of Witchcraft!" as he attacks his former lover.

The Succubus attack was unrelated.

The party may roleplay downtime and level up before they move on to the next adventure.

CREATURES

NOBLES.

If the players decide to attack any of the guests during this session, or even Duke Reylander himself, you may use the following statblock.

If the party manages to attack the Succubus before she disappears, she might command the Duke to attack the party. If the Duke is caught on his own, he will try to reach a bell pull (typically next to the mantelpiece). It would likely take 10 nobles to seriously threaten just one party member, so any combat between the players and the party guests would likely be short. It would derail the campaign somewhat, too, so hopefully they won't. If at all possible, attempt to resolve conflicts through roleplayed negotiation rather than resorting to a violent altercation.

Noble
Medium humanoid (any race), any alignment

Armor Class 15 (breastplate)
Hit Points 9 (2d8)
Speed 30 ft.

STR	DEX	CON	INT	WIS	CHA
11 (+0)	12 (+1)	11 (+0)	12 (+1)	14 (+2)	16 (+3)

Skills Deception +5, Insight +4, Persuasion +5
Senses passive Perception 12
Languages any two languages
Challenge 1/8 (25 XP)

Actions

Rapier. *Melee Weapon Attack:* +3 to hit, reach 5 ft., one target. *Hit:* 5 (1d8 + 1) piercing damage.

Reactions

Parry. The noble adds 2 to its AC against one melee attack that would hit it. To do so, the noble must see the attacker and be wielding a melee weapon.

SUCCUMBUS

The Succubus isn't great at hand-to-hand combat. Her appearance here is something of a red herring, as well as providing a good reason for Duke Reylander to not be involved in the witch-hunt sessions directly. When the party realises what she is, have the Succubus use her Etherealness ability to disappear into the ethereal plane, but if the party manages to prevent her from doing this or has the ability to pursue her, have her use her Charm ability and try to get away again. Only use her Draining Kiss ability if they leave her no other choice. That ability has the potential to be lethal. Try not to kill the party's healer!

Succubus/Incubus
Medium fiend (shapechanger), neutral evil

Armor Class 15 (natural armor)
Hit Points 66 (12d8 + 12)
Speed 30 ft., fly 60 ft.

STR	DEX	CON	INT	WIS	CHA
8 (-1)	17 (+3)	13 (+1)	15 (+2)	12 (+1)	20 (+5)

Skills Deception +9, Insight +5, Perception +5, Persuasion +9, Stealth +7
Damage Resistances cold, fire, lightning, poison; bludgeoning, piercing, and slashing from nonmagical weapons
Senses darkvision 60 ft., passive Perception 15
Languages Abyssal, Common, Infernal, telepathy 60 ft.
Challenge 4 (1,100 XP)

Telepathic Bond. The fiend ignores the range restriction on its telepathy when communicating with a creature it has charmed. The two don't even need to be on the same plane of existence.

Shapechanger. The fiend can use its action to polymorph into a Small or Medium humanoid, or back into its true form. Without wings, the fiend loses its flying speed. Other than its size and speed, its statistics are the same in each form. Any equipment it is wearing or carrying isn't transformed. It reverts to its true form if it dies.

Actions

Claw (Fiend Form Only). *Melee Weapon Attack:* +5 to hit, reach 5 ft., one target. *Hit:* 6 (1d6 + 3) slashing damage.

Charm. One humanoid the fiend can see within 30 feet of it must succeed on a DC 15 Wisdom saving throw or be magically charmed for 1 day. The charmed target obeys the fiend's verbal or telepathic commands. If the target suffers any harm or receives a suicidal command, it can repeat the saving throw, ending the effect on a success. If the target successfully saves against the effect, or if the effect on it ends, the target is immune to this fiend's Charm for the next 24 hours.
The fiend can have only one target charmed at a time. If it charms another, the effect on the previous target ends.

Draining Kiss. The fiend kisses a creature charmed by it or a willing creature. The target must make a DC 15 Constitution saving throw against this magic, taking 32 (5d10 + 5) psychic damage on a failed save, or half as much damage on a successful one. The target's hit point maximum is reduced by an amount equal to the damage taken. This reduction lasts until the target finishes a long rest. The target dies if this effect reduces its hit point maximum to 0.

Etherealness. The fiend magically enters the Ethereal Plane from the Material Plane, or vice versa.

DIRE WOLVES.

A pair of Dire Wolves should be enough to cause trouble for the party. If the party finds the fight too easy, and you feel the need to buy time before the green hags' encounter, you might want to have another Dire Wolf or two come out of the woods.

Dire Wolf
Large beast, unaligned

Armor Class 14 (natural armor)
Hit Points 37 (5d10 + 10)
Speed 50 ft.

STR	DEX	CON	INT	WIS	CHA
17 (+3)	15 (+2)	15 (+2)	3 (-4)	12 (+1)	7 (-2)

Skills Perception +3, Stealth +4
Senses passive Perception 13
Languages —
Challenge 1 (200 XP)

Keen Hearing and Smell. The wolf has advantage on Wisdom (Perception) checks that rely on hearing or smell.

Pack Tactics. The wolf has advantage on an attack roll against a creature if at least one of the wolf's allies is within 5 ft. of the creature and the ally isn't incapacitated.

Actions

Bite. *Melee Weapon Attack:* +5 to hit, reach 5 ft., one target. *Hit:* 10 (2d6 + 3) piercing damage. If the target is a creature, it must succeed on a DC 13 Strength saving throw or be knocked prone.

THE 3 HAGS.

When the party discovers the hags and chooses to engage them in combat, decide which of the three is the Crone and try to have that be the one that receives the most damage from the party. As she comes close to losing the last of her hit points, have her finish herself off, spilling her blood over Beatrice and completing the ritual. Describe her body becoming bent and crooked, her arms and fingers elongating, her features distorting and her skin turning green as Beatrice becomes the new Maiden, the former Maiden becomes the new Mother, and the former Mother fills the role of Crone. This new group of three hags will then try to escape, cackling madly as they go, likely using their Invisible Passage feature. Hopefully, the encounter with the Dire Wolves will have already left the party unwilling to prolong this encounter, but as long as at least one of the hags gets away, then they will be available for the later adventure.

Green Hag

Medium fey, neutral evil

Armor Class 17 (natural armor)
Hit Points 82 (11d8 + 33)
Speed 30 ft.

STR	DEX	CON	INT	WIS	CHA
18 (+4)	12 (+1)	16 (+3)	13 (+1)	14 (+2)	14 (+2)

Skills Arcana +3, Deception +4, Perception +4, Stealth +3
Senses darkvision 60 ft., passive Perception 14
Languages Common, Draconic, Sylvan
Challenge 3 (700 XP)

Amphibious. The hag can breathe air and water.

Innate Spellcasting. The hag's innate spellcasting ability is Charisma (spell save DC 12). She can innately cast the following spells, requiring no material components:

At will: *dancing lights, minor illusion, vicious mockery*

Mimicry. The hag can mimic animal sounds and humanoid voices. A creature that hears the sounds can tell they are imitations with a successful DC 14 Wisdom (Insight) check.

Hag Coven. When hags must work together, they form covens, in spite of their selfish natures. A coven is made up of hags of any type, all of whom are equals within the group. However, each of the hags continues to desire more personal power.

A coven consists of three hags so that any arguments between two hags can be settled by the third. If more than three hags ever come together, as might happen if two covens come into conflict, the result is usually chaos.

Shared Spellcasting (Coven Only). While all three members of a hag coven are within 30 feet of one another, they can each cast the following spells from the wizard's spell list but must share the spell slots among themselves:

1st level (4 slots): *identify, ray of sickness*
2nd level (3 slots): *hold person, locate object*
3rd level (3 slots): *bestow curse, counterspell, lightning bolt*
4th level (3 slots): *phantasmal killer, polymorph*
5th level (2 slots): *contact other plane, scrying*
6th level (1 slot): *eye bite*

For casting these spells, each hag is a 12th-level spellcaster that uses Intelligence as her spellcasting ability. The spell save DC is 12+the hag's Intelligence modifier, and the spell attack bonus is 4+the hag's Intelligence modifier.

Hag Eye (Coven Only). A hag coven can craft a magic item called a hag eye, which is made from a real eye coated in varnish and often fitted to a pendant or other wearable item. The hag eye is usually entrusted to a minion for safekeeping and transport. A hag in the coven can take an action to see what the hag eye sees if the hag eye is on the same plane of existence. A hag eye has AC 10, 1 hit point, and darkvision with a radius of 60 feet. If it is destroyed, each coven member takes 3d10 psychic damage and is blinded for 24 hours.

A hag coven can have only one hag eye at a time, and creating a new one requires all three members of the coven to perform a ritual. The ritual takes 1 hour, and the hags can't perform it while blinded. During the ritual, if the hags take any action other than performing the ritual, they must start over.

Actions

Claws. *Melee Weapon Attack:* +6 to hit, reach 5 ft., one target. *Hit:* 13 (2d8 + 4) slashing damage.

Illusory Appearance. The hag covers herself and anything she is wearing or carrying with a magical illusion that makes her look like another creature of her general size and humanoid shape. The illusion ends if the hag takes a bonus action to end it or if she dies.

The changes wrought by this effect fail to hold up to physical inspection. For example, the hag could appear to have smooth skin, but someone touching her would feel her rough flesh. Otherwise, a creature must take an action to visually inspect the illusion and succeed on a DC 20 Intelligence (Investigation) check to discern that the hag is disguised.

Invisible Passage. The hag magically turns invisible until she attacks or casts a spell, or until her concentration ends (as if concentrating on a spell). While invisible, she leaves no physical evidence of her passage, so she can be tracked only by magic. Any equipment she wears or carries is invisible with her.

NAME

CLASS & LVL

RACE

BACKGROUND

PLAYER NAME GENDER

CURRENT HP   TEMP HP

EYES & HAIR   AGE

ALIGNMENT   EXP

MAX HP   HIT DIE

SKIN   HEIGHT & WEIGHT

INSPIRATION

PROFICIENCY BONUS

PASSIVE WISDOM

PERSONALITY TRAITS:

SAVING THROWS
- ○ ___ STRENGTH
- ○ ___ DEXTERITY
- ○ ___ CONSTITUTION
- ○ ___ INTELLIGENCE
- ○ ___ WISDOM
- ○ ___ CHARISMA

STR

SUCCESSES
FAILURES

DEATH SAVES

IDEALS:

DEX

AC   INIT   SP

BONDS:

SKILLS
- ○ ___ ACROBATICS DEX
- ○ ___ ANIMAL HANDLING WIS
- ○ ___ ARCANA INT
- ○ ___ ATHLETICS STR
- ○ ___ DECEPTION CHA
- ○ ___ HISTORY INT
- ○ ___ INSIGHT WIS
- ○ ___ INTIMIDATION CHA
- ○ ___ INVESTIGATION INT
- ○ ___ MEDICINE WIS
- ○ ___ NATURE INT
- ○ ___ PERCEPTION WIS
- ○ ___ PERFORMANCE CHA
- ○ ___ PERSUASION CHA
- ○ ___ RELIGION INT
- ○ ___ SLEIGHT OF HAND DEX
- ○ ___ STEALTH DEX
- ○ ___ SURVIVAL WIS

CON

INT

WIS

CHA

FLAWS:

ATTACKS & SPELLCASTING
NAME   ATK   DAMAGE/TYPE

FEATURES & TRAITS

OTHER PROFICIENCIES & LANGUAGES

EQUIPMENT

CP
SP
EP
GP
PP

CHARACTER APPEARANCE

CHARACTER BACKSTORY

DARK GIFTS

ADDITIONAL FEATURES & TRAITS

ALLIES & ORGANIZATIONS

SYMBOL

TREASURE

SP CASTING CLASS | SP ATK BONUS

SP CASTING ABILITY | SP SAVE DC

0 CANTRIPS

1

2

3

4

5

6

7

8

9

I HOPE YOU ENJOYED READING MY STORY! EPIC THANK YOU TO ALL MY KICKSTARTER BACKERS:

Cynthia Coffman ~ Deborah Hedges ~ Martin Průcha ~ Vesala ~ Deborah Snowden ~ Jack ~ i0m ~ Amanda Sabattis ~ Serena Mire ~ Jonathan Rust ~ lukecd ~ Angie Watson ~ Sean Christopher Charles Richer ~ Julie ~ Bendideia Publishing ~ Andreas Loeckher ~ Caleb Slama ~ Apaphous ~ Xingkai Zhao ~ kassandra ~ WizardFlight ~ Lorene Verity ~ Asher Bosworth ~ Dzekap ~ Aaron ~ Steven Byrd ~ GB ~ Onyx Santiago ~ Jeffrey Maynard ~ Judith Mortimore ~ Benjamin Kellett ~ Black Baron ~ Chris Perrin ~ Warf ~ Zane Bergman ~ Mike Bregel ~ Bruce ~ RJHopkinson ~ Katrina Grosskopf ~ Brittany Thompson ~ Haleigh ~ Sean ~ JLea ~ Katy ~ Alisha Klapheke ~ Melissa Daniels ~ Daniel Levine ~ Christina ~ Scott ~ The Creative Fund by BackerKit ~ Wolframsmith, LLC ~ Julie Feldskov ~ enriksen ~ Luna ~ Chad Kirkendall ~ Stephane Gelgoot ~ Jason Chartier ~ Andy ~ Sean ~ Daniel Gregory ~ Francis Launay ~ Tom Goodchild ~ Raven ~ Jenny Reed ~ Ken Hillier ~ Saz ~ Kaitlin Blaker ~ Lauren Williams ~ Johan Dijkshoorn ~ Raf Bressel ~ Trent Revis ~ michael haley ~ maileguy ~ Julie Alviar ~ Tuebor ~ Bridgette M. Findley ~ Jon Terry ~ Benjamin P. Powell ~ axolotl ~ Christian Kjærgaard

About the Author

In a small town in South Wales, I discovered magic...

I graduated from Swansea University with a bachelor's degree in American Studies in 2011. Yet, it wasn't my degree that sparked my imagination, but the magic of Harry Potter. If you're anything like me, then you, too, spent hours devouring everything you could find from that world. I surely did. And when the books ran out, I knew I wanted to write my own.

As a USA Today bestselling author, I've been crafting stories that readers love. These tales of sexy men and magic, including vampires, fae, and witches, consistently rise up the ranks on major retailers, such as Amazon and Apple.

One of my older books, Wyvern Awakening (Mage Chronicles Books 1), became an instant hit, and was nominated for the Kindle Storyteller Award in 2017. Passionate about paranormal and fantasy books, when I combined the magic of Harry Potter with the world of the Witcher Sagas and Slavic mythology, I knew deep down that readers would love my Baba-Yaga-inspired series.

Over the past year, I've been reading everything I could on Slavic Mythology. I researched Baba Yaga, the famous Slavic witch from folklore. You see, I was determined to come up with my own version based of Slavic myths and legends.

A story was born that still stoked the fires I knew my readers loved. I was so passionate about this world and story, I finished writing the first draft of Witch's Rose in three months, and now book 2 is in the editing phase as well.

Born in Poland, I've lived in the UK for the past 16 years and enjoy writing about Alpha Males, spicy tales, and things that make my heart happy. So if you love heat, strong females, and thick books, this will surely delight you, too.

Made in the USA
Columbia, SC
04 May 2023

804fff60-560b-450d-bea6-3de279c639a9R01